DATE DUE JUL 04

MAY 03 05

THE
MYSTERIOUS
MERRY-GO-ROUND

Also by Marilyn Prather
in Large Print:

A Deadly Reunion
A Light in the Darkness

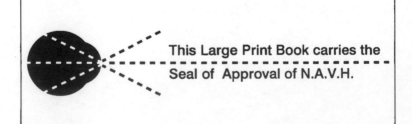

This Large Print Book carries the
Seal of Approval of N.A.V.H.

THE
MYSTERIOUS
MERRY-GO-ROUND

MARILYN PRATHER

Thorndike Press • Waterville, Maine

Published in 2004 by arrangement with Marilyn Prather.

Thorndike Press® Large Print Candlelight.

The tree indicium is a trademark of Thorndike Press.

The text of this Large Print edition is unabridged. Other aspects of the book may vary from the original edition.

Set in 16 pt. Plantin by Ramona Watson.

Printed in the United States on permanent paper.

Library of Congress Cataloging-in-Publication Data

Prather, Marilyn.
    The mysterious merry-go-round / Marilyn Prather.
        p. cm.
    ISBN 0-7862-6553-1 (lg. print : hc : alk. paper)
    1. Inheritance and succession — Fiction.   2. Home ownership — Fiction.   3. Merry-go-round — Fiction.
    4. Large type books.   I. Title.
    PS3566.R273M975 2004
    813′.54—dc22   2004045981

To all the great poets who have
inspired me with their words.

I stand by the river where both of us stood,
And there is but one shadow to darken the
    flood;
And the path leading to it, where both used
    to pass,
Has the step of but one to take dew from the
    grass.
    One forlorn since that day.

Go, be sure of my love, by that treason
    forgiven;
Of my prayers, by the blessings they win thee
    from heaven;
Of my grief (guess the length of the sword by
    the sheath's);
By the silence of life, more pathetic than
    death's!
    Go, — be clear of that day!

                    — From "That Day" by
                    Elizabeth Barrett Browning

As the Founder/CEO of NAVH, the only national health agency solely devoted to those who, although not totally blind, have an eye disease which could lead to serious visual impairment, I am pleased to recognize Thorndike Press* as one of the leading publishers in the large print field.

Founded in 1954 in San Francisco to prepare large print textbooks for partially seeing children, NAVH became the pioneer and standard setting agency in the preparation of large type.

Today, those publishers who meet our standards carry the prestigious "Seal of Approval" indicating high quality large print. We are delighted that Thorndike Press is one of the publishers whose titles meet these standards. We are also pleased to recognize the significant contribution Thorndike Press is making in this important and growing field.

Lorraine H. Marchi, L.H.D.
Founder/CEO
NAVH

* Thorndike Press encompasses the following imprints: Thorndike, Wheeler, Walker and Large Pr int Press.

Chapter One

Ariele Harwood pulled her Honda into the last available parking space along Larkspur's winding Main Street. As fortune would have it, the space happened to be right in front of the building that housed the law offices of Cyril Vance Caulfield III.

Ariele got out of her car and searched her purse for dimes. As she began to feed the parking meter, her eyes strayed to the sleek silver Mercedes that occupied the space to her left. She imagined the car belonged to the attorney. Then her gaze slid to the motorcycle parked on the other side of her Honda. It was without a doubt one of the gaudiest motorcycles she had ever seen.

She stared at it, frowning. It looked just like the one Jerod had owned. Once, the subject of motorcycles would have excited her. But that was back when she and Jerod were an item — before he had almost gotten them both killed on his bike while rounding a sharp curve at warp speed. Now she had a decided aversion to the machines.

Distracted, Ariele let the last dime slip from her fingers. It rolled onto the pavement and under the front tire of the motorcycle. *What luck,* she thought, bending to retrieve the dime. As she straightened, her arm hit against the tire and she felt the bike shimmy.

She glanced around, half expecting to see some brawny guy in leather and studs shaking his fists at her. But no one was there, and the bike didn't topple over as she'd feared it might. Ariele shoved the dime into the meter and headed quickly toward the building.

A young woman with straight blond hair was seated behind the receptionist's desk just inside the front door. She got up when Ariele walked in. "You're here for the reading of the Sheldrake will?" she asked.

Ariele noted that the receptionist was very attractive. And her long, shapely legs were shown off in a stunning way by the short, tight skirt she wore. Ariele felt instantly dumpy and disheveled by comparison. Her hand went to her hair, smoothing back a wayward strand that had fallen over her cheek. "Yes," she said at last. "I'm Ariele Harwood."

The receptionist gave her a cool smile. "Please come with me." She led Ariele down a hall to the last door. "In here," she said. "Mr. Caulfield'll be with you soon."

Ariele thanked her and stepped into a small room that boasted a massive oak table and matching chairs. But it wasn't the furniture that caught her attention. It was the two women who sat side by side at the table.

Ariele recognized them immediately. They were Elizabeth Sheldrake's half-sisters. Their mother had been Elizabeth's stepmother. Ariele had met them a few years before at the wedding of a mutual acquaintance in Poughkeepsie. She couldn't recall their names, but she remembered their pinched-looking faces and how imposing they had seemed, even then. And she remembered the identical mops of gray curls that circled their heads like caps that fit too tight.

She remembered their eyes too, the manner in which they had stared, dark and piercing, into hers, as if they were trying to probe inside her mind. They stared at her the same way now. And Ariele's response was the same as it had been then. She felt uneasy.

The only feature that set the two women apart was their weight. One was thin, the other stout.

9

Conscious that the sisters were watching her, Ariele took a seat on the opposite side of the table. She knew they must be asking themselves why she had been called to the reading of the will. She had asked herself the same question ever since she'd received the letter informing her she'd been named an heir in her great-aunt's estate.

It didn't take a genius to figure out that the sisters stood to inherit the estate itself. Daring to meet their eyes, Ariele attempted a smile. "Hello. I'm Ariele Harwood," she said. "I believe we met at Grace Linwold's wedding."

The thin sister sniffed and drew herself up so that she looked even more angular. "I'm afraid I don't remember. Do you, Blanche?"

Blanche's eyes narrowed. "No, Zelda, but then I've always said that your memory is much keener than mine."

Ariele suspected the sisters were lying, but she wasn't about to press the subject. A strained silence fell over the room, and she wished that the attorney would come.

Just then the door opened. A short, balding man in an ill-fitting suit bustled into the room, wheezing as he walked. Ariele knew it wasn't polite, but she couldn't help watching him. *This* was Cyril

Vance Caulfield III? The name had conjured in Ariele's mind images of a tall, urbane man with sharp eyes and sleek hair that showed a hint of gray around the temples, a man whose dignified appearance matched that of the silver Mercedes.

Instead of taking the chair at the head of the table, as Ariele might have expected, the man plopped down in the one beside her. He gave another wheeze, then turned to her. "What a relief," he declared, running a hand over the hairless part of his head. "I thought for sure I was going to be late."

It seemed an odd thing for the attorney to say, but Ariele gave him a polite smile. "We haven't been waiting long, Mr. Caulfield." Too late she realized the "we" included Zelda and Blanche.

The man laughed heartily; his cheeks turned a rosy color. "You think I'm Mr. Caulfield?"

Ariele's face warmed uncomfortably. "But . . . you're not?"

"No. I'm Philip Hubbard, president of the Larkspur Historical Society," he said, with emphasis on the word *president*. He gave his attention to the sisters. "Zelda. Blanche. You're looking well today."

Ariele decided that Philip Hubbard was

11

something of a flatterer. But she saw that his words had a desirable effect on the sisters. Their mouths twitched into what might be considered smiles.

"We're well, thank you, Philip," Zelda replied. "Quite well." Her steady gaze settled on Ariele again.

Philip gave a small chuckle. "And it seems Mr. Caulfield's picked a great day for . . ." He never finished his sentence.

The door opened again; all heads, Ariele's included, turned toward it. A man strode in, carrying an attaché case. Ariele knew the man had to be Cyril Vance Caulfield III, but her surprise over his appearance was just as great as when she'd mistaken Philip Hubbard for the attorney.

To begin with, Mr. Caulfield had coppery red hair — which, Ariele was bound to note, was set off in a striking way by the white dress shirt and blue-and-black striped tie that he wore. He was young too, somewhere in his thirties, she estimated. He must be around six feet tall, and he was well built and good-looking, in an unconventional sort of way. But it wasn't his age or his height or his other assets that riveted Ariele's attention and made her eyes widen.

It was his pants. They were black and shiny and made of leather.

A lawyer who wore leather to the office? Ariele tore her gaze from the pants and the disconcerting way they clung to the attorney's legs. She wondered if he had seen her interest in his clothing. She fervently hoped not. But what about the sisters? Were they shocked too?

Glancing in their direction, Ariele hid a smile. The sisters' faces were more pinched-looking than ever. Her eyes slid back to the attorney. At once she thought of the motorcycle parked outside. She had a strong suspicion that it belonged to Mr. Caulfield.

But if the motorcycle was the attorney's, then who owned the Mercedes? Was it Zelda? Or maybe Blanche? Somehow, Philip Hubbard didn't strike Ariele as the type who would tool around Larkspur in a fancy car.

Ariele had no more time to debate the matter of vehicles and their owners. The attorney had taken his chair at the head of the table.

"Sorry I'm late." He offered what struck Ariele as a self-assured smile. His gaze swept around the table. When his eyes met Ariele's, they held hers for an amazingly long time. "I hope I didn't inconvenience anyone," he said.

Even as she told herself that she didn't like Mr. Caulfield's demeanor, that he reminded her too much of Jerod, Ariele found herself staring back into his extraordinarily blue eyes. They commanded her attention, and it occurred to her that they must be a great help to the attorney in convincing skeptical jurors to see things his way. "You didn't," she said at last, though his remark had obviously been rhetorical.

Embarrassed, Ariele averted her eyes, but her ears picked up the attorney's softly spoken "Good." Then she heard a snapping sound and she dared a look up again. Mr. Caulfield was opening his briefcase.

His face was hidden from her as he took out a long sheet of paper from the case and laid it on the table in front of him. Was Mr. Caulfield one of those men with inflated egos who took it for granted that every female was irresistibly drawn to him? Jerod had been like that; never mind that she had at one time found him enormously attractive. She didn't date men like Jerod anymore. Of the several men she saw casually now, she was happy to say that none of them was egotistical. None of them was particularly exciting company, either, she had to admit. But that was all right with her.

"Why don't we proceed," Mr. Caulfield said, breaking into Ariele's thoughts in a most businesslike manner. She was forced to put away any notions she might have about his ego or his sex appeal.

A quick glance across the table told Ariele that the attorney had the complete interest of everyone in the room. The sisters and Philip Hubbard were leaning forward, their heads tilted in almost identical poses.

"As you're all aware," Mr. Caulfield began, "you were called here this afternoon because you have been named as beneficiaries in Elizabeth Sheldrake's will." His gaze took in the small group again.

Then he cleared his throat and bent his head over the piece of paper. " 'This is the Last Will and Testament of Elizabeth Irene Sheldrake. I, Elizabeth Irene Sheldrake, being of sound mind, and residing at Sheldrake Manor, Burroughs Lane, County of Burroughs, State of New York, declare that this is my Last Will and Testament and I revoke all previous wills and codicils.' "

The attorney paused. Zelda sniffed and Blanche let out a long, tremulous sigh.

Ariele's heart gave a couple of wild thumps. She was surprised at her reaction, since she had no real reason to get excited. She had barely known her great-aunt, had met her just once, and that had been many years ago when she and her mother had paid a visit to Sheldrake. All she could remember of the visit was that the manor had impressed her as huge and ancient and a bit mysterious, and Elizabeth Sheldrake seemed old and fragile-looking, though she had told Ariele in a crisp, clear voice to call her just "Aunt Elizabeth."

Mr. Caulfield went on reading: " 'I have never been married and I have no children or grandchildren. I make the following specific gifts. I give my brass candelabra, my walnut curio cabinet, and collections of Peach Blow and cut crystal inkwells to the Larkspur Historical Society.' " He glanced at Philip Hubbard.

Ariele noted that the president of the Historical Society had gone red in the face. He gave a stiff nod of acknowledgment in Mr. Caulfield's direction. Before Ariele could gauge the sisters' reaction, the attorney had resumed his reading.

" 'I give my cameo brooch, my chestnut sideboard with carved wolf's head, and my Baldwin piano and entire collection of sheet music to Zelda Pilchard, who is my half-sister by way of my father, Samuel's, marriage to Grace Pilchard.' "

There was a loud gasp from the sisters' side of the table. Mr. Caulfield continued, " 'I give my diamond and pearl flower spray brooch, my jam cupboard and matching dining table, and six Windsor chairs to Blanche Pilchard, who is my half-sister by way of . . .' "

An "Oh dear, no," which Ariele attributed to Blanche, drowned out the attorney's next words. Ariele couldn't blame the woman. A jam cupboard. A table. If the items had gone to her, Ariele knew that neither she nor the sisters would have been shocked. But did that mean Elizabeth Sheldrake had left the bulk of her estate to someone other than Zelda or Blanche? Maybe a separate provision named the sisters as joint heirs.

A discreet cough from the attorney drew Ariele's eyes back to him. His mouth twitched up in a smile. When he seemed satisfied that he had her undivided attention, he looked down at the will.

" 'I give all the rest of my property, Sheldrake Manor and estate, and any cash, stocks, and bonds as may be remaining to Ariele Harwood, who is my great-niece by way of . . .' "

At the mention of her name, there were three loud gasps. One, Ariele realized, was her own. The other two must have come from the sisters' mouths. Waves of disbelief and shock swept through Ariele. A sense of numbness settled in her bones, and her vision blurred for a moment so that she couldn't see the expressions of those seated around her.

But she did realize something. The fiery-haired lawyer with the pompous-sounding name had made a terrible error. He had wrongly stated that she, Ariele Harwood, had just inherited Elizabeth Sheldrake's estate, when what he had meant to say was that Zelda and Blanche Pilchard were the rightful heirs of the property, as well as their half-sister's " 'cash, stocks, and bonds as may be remaining.' "

Ariele sought to clear her mind of its confusion, to form a protest that would straighten out the matter of who had inherited what. Before she could trust herself to speak, she heard another voice sharply address the attorney. It belonged to Zelda. Ariele blinked and Zelda came into focus. She stood facing Mr. Caulfield, tall and imperious.

"Mr. Caulfield," she repeated, half stumbling on the name, "you are wrong, entirely wrong."

"Wrong?"

"Most assuredly." Zelda drew herself up to the full length of her bony height. "Our dear sister Elizabeth would never entrust her beloved Sheldrake to anyone but myself and Blanche."

At the mention of her name, Blanche rose from her chair. Her face was flushed crimson in color — whether from confusion or outrage, Ariele couldn't be sure.

"That's right, Mr. Caulfield," Blanche began in a quavering voice. "Our Elizabeth . . . God rest her dear soul . . . as good as told us on her . . . sickbed . . ." Blanche choked on the word. "Forgive me." She bowed her head. Pulling a tissue from her dress pocket, she dabbed at her eyes with it. The gesture seemed to help her regain her composure. "Elizabeth said that she wanted Sheldrake to go to someone who would take proper care of it."

"And you interpreted that to mean yourself or Zelda?"

Blanche braced herself against the table. But instead of answering the attorney, she looked at Zelda, as if she were uncertain. Ariele assumed that Zelda acted as spokeswoman for the pair.

19

"I hardly think, Mr. Caulfield, that this is a matter of . . . of interpretation," Zelda spluttered. "Who else could Elizabeth possibly have meant?" She threw her arms in the air. The next instant she set her steely eyes on Ariele.

Zelda's gaze was defiant; it dared Ariele to rise and defend herself. Perhaps she suspected that Ariele had already known about the provision. But there was nothing that Ariele knew to say, nor was she about to get into a verbal sparring match with Zelda Pilchard. She sent the attorney a silent appeal for help. After all, wasn't he in charge here?

He telegraphed her a smile that seemed to say he had everything under control. Then he rose from his chair and faced Zelda, his hands planted firmly on the table. "Miss Pilchard, I assure you that the provisions of Elizabeth Sheldrake's will are in complete accord with her wishes. Now I'll have to ask you to sit down and allow me to continue without further interruption. Your other choice is to leave the room."

Zelda stared at him, mouth open, a stunned look on her face. She stood still for a moment, as if she might challenge him. Then she sat down, and Blanche followed her lead.

Ariele thought she saw a touch of smugness in the attorney's expression, as if he savored his little triumph over the Pilchard sisters. And if she were truthful, she'd have to say she was enjoying it too. Preoccupied with her thoughts, Ariele missed most of the conclusion of the reading. There was something about the attorney himself being appointed executor of the estate. And there was a declaration that Elizabeth Sheldrake had signed her Last Will and Testament " 'freely, under no constraint or undue influence.' "

Then it was over and Mr. Caulfield was on his feet. The others got up. Finally, Ariele rose too.

"Miss Harwood, I'd like to see you privately in my office."

Ariele realized the attorney had spoken to her. "Yes, of course, Mr. Caulfield," she said automatically. She wondered what effect his request would have on Zelda and Blanche.

But it was Philip Hubbard who spoke. "Miss Harwood." She turned in his direction. He gave her a pleasant smile as he took something from his wallet. "My business card," he explained, handing it to her. "If you would give me a call, I'd like to make arrangements with you to pick up the items Miss Sheldrake left to the Historical Society."

"That won't be needed," the attorney put in before Ariele could respond. "I'll be handling the necessary arrangements. Phone my office, Philip, and we'll set up a time."

The smile faded from the man's face. Ariele thought that he looked disappointed, though he bobbed his head at the attorney and said, "All right."

The sisters were a different matter. Their faces wore sullen expressions, and Zelda stood with her arms crossed over her flat chest. "You can rest assured, Mr. Caulfield, that you'll be hearing from our attorney. We have no intention of letting this farce continue." She sniffed again as her icy gaze took in Ariele.

Ariele nearly spoke up then and told the attorney that she didn't want Sheldrake, that he should change the will and give the property to the Pilchard sisters, whether they were entitled to it or not. But she couldn't get the words out — not with Zelda and Blanche present. Besides, she doubted the will could be changed. Her only choice at the moment was to turn away from Zelda's penetrating stare.

The sisters left the room first. Fast on

their heels was Philip Hubbard, and Ariele suddenly found herself alone with the attorney.

"If you'll come with me, Miss Harwood, the keys to the manor are in my desk, along with papers that you'll need to sign, though there won't be time for that today." He gave her that same self-confident smile.

The smile must be his stock in trade, Ariele decided. That, and his eyes, which momentarily captured hers before he turned and led her down the hallway.

The attorney opened a door at the end and motioned for Ariele to go in. She saw that his office contained a desk piled with papers. A chair was barely visible behind the desk. By the door was a bookcase crammed with books. Two upholstered chairs were situated beside the desk. Mr. Caulfield motioned with his hand for Ariele to take one of them.

As she settled herself in the chair, her eyes went to several framed photographs that decorated the wall behind the desk. Two were prints of motorcycles, but the third was something entirely different. It was a photograph of a butterfly, an unusually striking specimen, with wings the same color as the attorney's eyes.

"That's a Blackburn's Bluet."

Ariele started at the close sound of Mr. Caulfield's voice. Turning, she found him standing beside her. His hand rested on the wide arm of the chair, and he leaned over until his face was on a level with hers. "It's a beautiful specimen, don't you think?"

For some reason, her gaze strayed more to the attorney than the butterfly. "Yes . . . fantastic," she had to agree.

"And it's native only to the Hawaiian Islands."

"Really?" Why was Mr. Caulfield bothering to tell her about an insect? And why was he standing so near? Maybe the print was a conversation piece he used to put his clients at ease. If so, it was having the opposite effect on her.

All at once the attorney straightened and gave a small laugh. "I'm sure you're a lot more anxious to see your new estate than to discuss butterflies." He went around to the other side of the desk and sat down. Then he opened a drawer and took out a set of keys.

Ariele watched him as he laid the keys out on the desk. "I'm afraid, Mr. Caulfield, that I'm in kind of a state of shock. I hardly knew my aunt. I can't imagine why she left her estate to me."

The attorney appeared slightly amused. "It seems, Miss Harwood, that your aunt must have known you better than you knew her. She made you an heiress."

Ariele had to laugh at the term, but the whole idea was too bizarre, foreign to her. "It's like I'm dreaming. This isn't real."

"Believe me, you're not dreaming, Miss Harwood. If you don't mind my asking, what do you do for a living?"

"I'm a librarian at a community college."

The attorney smiled. "Well, now you're a librarian who owns a twelve-room manor and fifty acres."

A knot formed in Ariele's stomach. Was it caused by excitement — or dread? And if it was true that she wasn't dreaming, just what was she going to do with a decrepit Victorian mansion whose gardens and grounds, as she vaguely recalled, were overgrown with weeds and high grass?

Ariele laughed again, a nervous laugh. Her eyes flitted to the butterfly print; its ethereal beauty calmed her briefly. "I can understand why the Pilchard sisters were so upset. They must feel very cheated since they came here expecting to inherit the house." Her eyes returned to Mr. Caulfield's. "That's what I was expecting too — for them to inherit Sheldrake, I mean."

"But you're the owner instead." His expression suddenly changed; he looked irritated. "Don't lose sleep feeling sorry for Zelda and Blanche," he said abruptly.

His remark made Ariele question whether she felt actual sympathy for the disagreeable sisters. She had to conclude that she didn't.

Mr. Caulfield came to the other side of the desk, keys in hand. He perched himself on the corner nearest Ariele. "Don't be fooled by the sisters, either," he said. "They've got enough money to keep them in the manner to which they're accustomed." His face relaxed. "Which is to say, they're loaded."

Ariele didn't reply, but she knew that people who were "loaded" could still be greedy for more. She wondered too if the sisters' lifestyle included a Mercedes. Looking up, she was careful not to let her eyes rest on the attorney's leather-clad legs. "I got the impression they're going to put up a fight for Sheldrake."

He shrugged. "Let them. They'll just line their lawyer's pockets. Now . . ." He untangled his legs and slid off the desk. "Why don't we go out to see your estate?"

Ariele got up from her chair. He'd said "we." That meant he was going to take her there. She hesitated. "I want you to know I don't intend to keep Sheldrake."

Mr. Caulfield pinned her with his gaze. "Oh?"

Ariele felt foolish under his inspection. But why should she? Since the estate now belonged to her, she wasn't obligated to offer him, or anyone else, an explanation. "That's right. I'll be putting it up for sale," she said impulsively.

Those dazzling eyes narrowed a little. "How can you be sure that's what you want to do when you haven't seen the place yet?"

Ariele was tempted to tell him that she didn't need a grand tour of the manor — particularly if he was the one conducting it. Aware that he was waiting for her answer, she drew herself up to her full height, which was a great deal less than his. "I've seen Sheldrake. My mother took me there once to visit Aunt Elizabeth. It was the year before my mother died."

"I'm sorry," the attorney said, but that was all. Then he turned away from her and started for the door. He didn't look back, and Ariele had no choice but to go after him.

At the front desk, he stopped and said something to the receptionist that Ariele didn't catch. But she did see the way the receptionist's blond hair flowed over her shoulders when she tilted her head to look up at her boss.

The attorney gave his attention to Ariele. "Where's your car parked?"

"Just outside."

He held the door open for her, and she stepped from the office into the bright sunshine of an early summer afternoon.

"The blue Honda," Ariele indicated when the attorney came up beside her. She noted that the Mercedes was still there.

"You can follow me if you like, Miss Harwood," the attorney offered. "Or you could . . ."

"Van!" a masculine voice called.

Ariele turned in the direction of the voice. A man was approaching. He wore white shorts and a red shirt. When he stopped in front of them, Ariele realized that his eyes were on her instead of "Van," as he'd called the attorney.

Despite the fact that the man's gaze traveled over her in an uncomfortably thorough manner, Ariele saw that he was quite handsome, with black hair that lightly skimmed the collar of his shirt. There was an aura about him that hinted of money and power. Ariele estimated that he was a little older than Mr. Caulfield, and he stood half a head taller than the attorney.

"Archer."

The man shifted his gaze to Mr. Caulfield. There was tension in the air between the two men. Ariele felt it in the same way one feels electricity in the air before a storm.

Suddenly, the man's attention reverted to Ariele. "I give you credit, Van Caulfield," he said with a calculated smile. "You always manage to wind up with the most beautiful woman."

"You've got that one right, Archer."

Ariele's cheeks grew hot at the exchange. She didn't know whom she was more upset with, the attorney or the man called Archer. She determined to put them both in their places. Before she had the chance, she felt a hand at her elbow.

"Come on," the attorney said, steering her in the direction of the curb and away from Archer.

She glared up at him, but it was no use. His eyes were fixed straight ahead. As soon as they'd negotiated the curb, she pulled free from his grasp. "I can take care of myself, Mr. Caulfield," she said icily.

"I'm sure you can, Miss Harwood," he snapped.

Stung, Ariele watched with angry eyes as he strode over to the motorcycle and unzipped a saddlebag that was positioned behind the seat. He took out a pair of gloves and a black helmet that had a jagged blue stripe down each side. He fitted the helmet over his head, fastened the chin strap, and pulled the gloves onto his hands.

It was then that she noticed something written on the side of the cycle. "The Litigator," it said in bold red letters. *That figures,* Ariele thought. An attorney was bound to have more than a passing acquaintance with litigation.

He mounted the cycle and looked over at her. He grinned, as if he knew she'd been watching. "As I was saying when we were so rudely interrupted, you can follow me in your car. Or you can ride along on The Litigator. I keep an extra helmet in the office, just in case."

He must imagine that he was being clever. But Ariele fixed him with icy eyes, conveying without words that she didn't find his remark the least bit amusing. Mustering a polite smile, she said, "Thank you, but I wouldn't care to ruin my best suit." That much was true. The beige linen suit she wore was the nicest that she owned.

The attorney smiled disarmingly. "Well,

maybe another time when you're not so . . . dressed."

Fuming, Ariele got into her car, slamming the door harder than necessary. She considered Cyril Vance Caulfield III's conduct unbecoming to his profession — and worse. He reminded her more and more of Jerod. Maybe his attitude was the reason for the animosity between himself and the man named Archer. But, recalling Archer's suggestive remarks, the manner in which his eyes had ranged over her from head to foot, she concluded that she liked him even less than the attorney.

Ariele heard The Litigator being coaxed to life beside her. She pretended not to notice. At once there was a horrendous roar, and she let out a startled cry, which she was sure the attorney would enjoy — if he could hear it. Sneaking a glance in his direction, she saw his head turned toward her. He lifted his hand and gave her a thumbs-up sign.

Ariele ignored the salute, choosing to give her attention to the Mercedes. But she found no respite there. Archer sat behind the wheel of the fancy car, his gaze glued on her.

Ariele jerked her head away. She thrust the key into the ignition and backed out of the parking space. But as she steered the Honda down Main Street, she couldn't shake the strange feeling that her path and Archer's would cross again, and she thought that if she had been the one to inherit the jam cupboard or the piano, she wouldn't have complained at all.

Chapter Two

The estate was located farther from town than Ariele had imagined. She had followed the attorney for perhaps five miles when he turned the motorcycle onto a gravel road. A wooden sign told her the road was Burroughs Lane. Bordering the lane on either side were tall, leafy bushes that blocked out the view beyond. Ariele felt as if she were in a tunnel, and it made her uneasy. She'd never been fond of confining spaces.

To her relief, the lane wasn't long. Rounding a curve, she saw the manor just ahead. The home sat in the midst of a huge yard, and with its gabled roof and latticework, it reminded Ariele of something out of a fairy tale. But on closer view, she saw the house looked more neglected than magnificent. Her heart sank. How could she ever hope to sell the place if it was in a deplorable condition?

The motorcycle came to a gravel-crunching halt in front of Ariele, and she had to brake hard to avoid hitting the bike's rear tire. Jumping out of her car, she folded her arms in front of her and sent the attorney a wilting glance.

Mr. Caulfield regarded her, one eyebrow cocked. Was he amused? He turned from her before she could decide, but she couldn't keep from watching as he removed his helmet and hung it over one of the handlebars of the bike. He took off his gloves and deposited them in the upside-down helmet. Then he smoothed his hair back with one hand. "Are you ready?" he asked, glancing her way.

Uncertainty replaced her indignation. "I don't know if I am or not."

The attorney smiled. "When you get a closer look at the estate, you're going to realize what a treasure it is."

His overconfident air irked Ariele all over again. Where did he come off anyway? He hadn't a clue about her, what she might consider a treasure. Yet he was determined that she would fall head over heels for the place. "It doesn't matter whether I like the estate or not, Mr. Caulfield, because I don't intend to keep it."

He put his hands on his hips. "I'm aware of that. You told me already."

In exasperation Ariele turned from him and started across the yard. Despite her agitation, she noticed the large lawn was nicely trimmed. So were the bushes skirting the house. Perhaps it was a sign that the house wasn't too poorly kept.

Mr. Caulfield caught up with her as she started up the steps that led onto the porch. The attorney touched her arm. "There's something I need to tell you."

"What?" she asked cautiously.

He appeared slightly abashed. "The estate comes with a housekeeper and gardener. Elizabeth left funds in a special account to take care of their salaries and household expenses for a few months. After that . . ."

"After that, the new owner is responsible," Ariele finished. "Right?"

Mr. Caulfield regarded her. "Only if the new owner decides to keep Sheldrake. Which I hope you will," he added stubbornly.

Ariele felt flustered under his gaze. She'd hardly been able to absorb the news that the estate was hers, let alone that she was responsible for two employees. Now she wondered why on earth her aunt had chosen this man to execute her will. Had he charmed his way into her graces? Or was he the only attorney to choose from in Larkspur?

The attorney in question reached for the

35

knocker on the door. Before he could lift it, the door swung open, revealing a plump, white-haired woman. She looked stern and proper in her white blouse, navy skirt, and starched apron. Ariele surmised the woman was the housekeeper.

"I've been expecting you, Mr. Caulfield," the woman said with a tight smile. Her eyes flicked over Ariele and the smile vanished.

"How have you been, Emma?" the attorney asked.

The woman continued to observe Ariele. "Fine. And you?"

"Never been better, thanks. I've brought Miss Harwood out to get acquainted with her estate."

Mr. Caulfield sounded solicitous, but Ariele felt uncomfortable under the housekeeper's scrutiny. "Come in," Emma said, though the invitation was far from cordial.

Ariele's first impression of the inside of the manor was of dark wood, shadowy corners, and the scent of lemon polish. She saw she stood in a foyer. Through the foyer, to the right, she spotted a staircase. Beside the stairs was a tall window draped in heavy lace. The effect reminded her of an old cathedral she'd once toured.

"Through here," Emma said. She led the

way into the hall. The corridor was poorly lit; it too gave Ariele the impression she was traveling through a tunnel.

Emma stopped in front of a closed door. "This is the front parlor," she announced, motioning for Ariele to go ahead of her.

Ariele glanced over her shoulder at Mr. Caulfield. He gave her what seemed to be an encouraging smile. One glimpse showed Ariele that the parlor was a marked contrast to the dingy foyer and hall. Sunlight streamed into the room through double glass doors, and the scene jogged a memory in her. She remembered this was the room where her aunt had served her and her mother tea and fancy cakes. The same matching rose-colored sofa and love seat still stood at angles to one another in the center of the room. But had there been vases of flowers too, as there were now? The blooms' sweet fragrance muted the smell of polish.

Spying the Baldwin piano in a corner of the parlor, Ariele went over to it. The instrument was lovely, constructed of some rich, dark wood, maybe walnut. Ariele ran her fingers admiringly over the closed keyboard.

"Do you play?"

She turned to find Mr. Caulfield next to

her. "I took lessons once when I was eight. But only for a year." She smiled, recalling how she'd struggled through her lessons with the grim-faced but patient Mrs. Sternholm as her teacher. "Do you, Mr. Caulfield?"

He laid his hand on the keyboard where hers had been. "Never learned a note. But you don't have to know how to read music to play this piano."

"What do you mean?"

"Haven't you ever heard of a player piano? And I'm not talking about one that's got a computerized keyboard."

She understood. "Yes, of course. Isn't there a box inside the piano where you put a rolled-up sheet of music or something?"

"Right here." Mr. Caulfield pulled open a little door on the instrument. It was empty. "I'll show you how it works another time."

"But the piano belongs to Zelda now."

The attorney sighed. "Yes, unfortunately."

In the background Emma cleared her throat. Ariele turned around. The house-keeper's expression told her that the new owner of Sheldrake wasn't winning any points with her by dawdling around a piano. "If you're ready, Miss Harwood, the library's through there." Emma indicated a sliding door pocketed in the wall.

On her way to join the housekeeper, Ariele passed the hearth. She couldn't help but notice the garish-looking clock that stood on the marble mantel.

"Aren't you sorry you didn't inherit it?"

Looking behind her, Ariele saw that Mr. Caulfield was smiling. "You mean the French mantel clock?" she asked innocently. "I'm sure it's much better suited to Zelda's tastes than to mine."

The attorney laughed. "Well, what you're about to see next is something that should be perfectly suited to your tastes."

Emma slid the door away on its track, revealing the library. As soon as she stepped into the room, Ariele detected a faint moldy smell. *Probably the place is full of old, crumbling books,* she thought to herself. But when Emma pulled back the drapes at the windows, Ariele forgot about the unpleasant odor. The library came alive with light, and she saw that its walls were lined with bookcases. Every case was filled with books.

The room was a librarian's secret dream. Ariele could hardly hold back the desire to rush over to the closest shelf and begin perusing the titles.

"Didn't I tell you that you'd love it?"

Mr. Caulfield posed the question very close to her ear, it seemed, and Ariele found herself staring up into his eyes. They were wide and bright with interest. "You didn't tell me there was a library, Mr. Caulfield."

"No, I thought that you would enjoy being surprised, Miss Harwood."

Surprised was hardly the word, and it dawned on Ariele that she had precious little space for books in her already cramped apartment back home. That meant she would have to take time to sort through the titles while she was here, see which ones she wanted to keep, which she might be able to part with. Or perhaps she could get her cousin Warren and his wife to help her box up the books and put them in storage. But where? Did she have the nerve to ask Warren to keep them for her too? He and his wife had a very small house.

"What do you think of your library, Miss Harwood?"

The attorney's question broke into her thoughts. "I guess I'm going to have to extend my stay in Larkspur by a few days," she said truthfully.

He looked pleased. "Good." He started to say something more, but Emma came forward.

"If you wouldn't mind, Mr. Caulfield, I need to get back to my cooking. I put a roast in the oven and I want to check on it."

"That's fine, Emma. I can take Miss Harwood upstairs, show her a few of the bedrooms."

The housekeeper regarded Ariele. "I hope you like roast beef and Yorkshire pudding, Miss Harwood."

Ariele loved roast beef, though she'd never had Yorkshire pudding. But did Emma mean that she was fixing the meal for her? "Yes . . . I do," she said at last, then realized that, by her admission, she had committed herself to eating dinner at Sheldrake.

"You'll be staying too, won't you, Mr. Caulfield?"

Ariele's eyes moved uneasily from Emma to the attorney. He looked regretful. "I wish I could. That is, if Miss Harwood wouldn't mind." He tossed Ariele an inquisitive glance. Turning back to Emma, he said, "But I'm afraid tonight's out. I've got a late appointment at the office. Another evening soon, though. I promise."

To her consternation, Ariele felt both relieved and disappointed. She envied the easy way he got out of the invitation. At

41

the same time, she considered that he might have proved to be interesting company.

"I've made up the guest room for tonight."

It was a moment before Ariele realized the housekeeper was talking to her. "I'm sorry."

Emma's mouth curved in a disapproving frown. "I was saying that I've made up the guest room for you. I've taken the dust sheets off the furniture in the mistress's suite too, if you'd rather sleep there."

At first Ariele was too stunned to respond. "I appreciate that, Emma, but I'm afraid I won't be . . ." She scolded herself for being timid. "What I mean is that I'll be going to a motel tonight."

Emma looked scornful. "I see. Very well then, I'll be on my way to the kitchen."

"Miss Harwood, you've got six bedrooms at your disposal. Why would you want to waste money on a motel?"

Mr. Caulfield's reasonable tone got under Ariele's skin even more than Emma's huffy one. She told herself to stay calm, that they were kidding themselves if they thought she was going to spend the night there alone.

When she didn't respond, the attorney

apparently chose to ignore her. "Go ahead," he told Emma. "We'll come by the kitchen after we're finished upstairs."

"All right." Emma directed a stiff nod at Ariele, then marched off down the hallway.

Ariele decided it was time that she stop letting some pushy lawyer make up her mind for her. As soon as she saw that Emma was gone, she confronted him. "I'm sorry if Emma will be insulted, but I'm not staying in the guest room tonight."

Her firmness only seemed to harden the attorney's determination. He planted his arms across his chest and stared at her. "That's your decision, but Emma's not going to understand. Frankly, neither do I."

"Maybe . . . Maybe I don't care, Mr. Caulfield." Ariele's cheeks felt on fire. She ducked her head so that he couldn't see her face.

But he was already ahead of her. "I think you do care. And furthermore, I think you're making another rash decision. How can you know you don't want to sleep in the guest room until you've seen it?"

Ariele could think of several valid reasons, but before she could tell him even one of them, the attorney had turned on his heel and strode ahead of her out of the library. By the time Ariele caught up with him, he was almost to the end of the corridor.

They mounted the stairs in silence, the only sound the tapping of Ariele's heels on the wooden steps. When he reached the top, the attorney flipped a switch on the wall; a pair of lamps flickered on. The light from them cast wavering shadows along the length of a hallway that looked identical to the one below.

"This should be a bedroom," Mr. Caulfield said. He opened a door on the right.

Ariele put on a smile, not wanting to give him the satisfaction of believing he had gotten under her skin. But the smile faded when she saw the room.

She supposed it was a bedroom, but with the furniture covered in dust sheets, she couldn't be sure. The air was stale, as if the room had been shut up for years. Maybe it had been, she considered, eyeing the peeling green paint on the walls and the waterspots on the ceiling. Were the spots an indication the roof leaked? She grimaced.

Mr. Caulfield gave a short laugh. "Most of the upstairs hasn't been used in a while."

"I guess not," she agreed dryly.

"Why don't we move on," he suggested.

44

They moved on, from one dreary bedroom to the next and to the two bathrooms that were on opposite sides of the hall from each other. Both looked as if they'd been renovated, with flower-patterned wallpaper and shiny tiled floors, though the claw-footed tubs and sinks were obviously old.

Mr. Caulfield turned on the faucets in the sink and tub in one of the bathrooms. "See? Hot and cold water," he said. Then he pulled the lever on the toilet and the water in it flushed away with a hearty gurgling sound.

Ariele smiled at the demonstration, relieved that the plumbing was in working order.

The attorney backtracked to a door that he'd skipped. "This is the guest room," he said.

"Oh," Ariele murmured as she stepped inside. The room was nothing like the other bedrooms. It looked lived in.

There was a canopy bed with a lacy white coverlet and plump pillows. Matching lace curtains hung at the room's two windows. A chest of drawers stood opposite the bed and there was a small nightstand that held a lamp and a telephone, as well as a vase of fresh daisies.

Ariele looked out one of the windows.

The porch roof was directly below her. Beyond that lay the vast front lawn, a lush rolling expanse of grass and trees and shrubs. The view was great, she had to concede.

The attorney came up beside her. "See why I told you not to make a hasty decision?"

Ariele looked sideways at him. "I have to admit that I'm surprised by the guest room."

"Then you'll stay at Sheldrake tonight."

Her eyes met his. "I didn't say that, Mr. Caulfield."

The corners of his mouth tilted in a smile. "Why don't you just call me Van. Everyone else does."

Van. That was the name the man called Archer had used. For a moment she said nothing, though her mind registered that he was standing too near again, and her nose picked up the spicy scent of his aftershave or cologne. Hadn't Jerod worn a similar scent? At last she said, "I suppose it wouldn't hurt for me to spend the night here and save some money on a motel."

"Emma will be glad that you're staying." Van paused. "Ariele — I assume I can call you that."

"Of course."

"I've got to get back to town soon, Ariele, so why don't we take a quick look at the last room. Actually, it's two rooms, the mistress's suite, as Emma called it." He led her to a door at the opposite end of the hall from the guest room.

Suite was the right word, Ariele decided on first sight of the elegant, if faded, rooms. A grand canopy bed held court in the center of the bedroom, though the rest of the furnishings consisted of just a bureau, a dressing table, and a couple of chairs. Several paintings, mostly woodland scenes, graced the flocked walls.

Ariele inspected the bed with its ivory satin spread and pillows in satin cases. Her aunt had slept there. *Had she died there too?* The thought gave Ariele a little chill.

Even if she had never gotten to know Elizabeth Sheldrake, she felt she wouldn't want to sleep in this room. The air seemed too cool, the atmosphere too dreary. The windows, with their heavy brocade draperies, faced north, which meant they didn't get the sun.

Ariele pushed aside one of the drapes and peered at the grounds below. The backyard was more immense, if anything, than the front lawn, and far wilder in appearance owing to the abundance of bushes and undergrowth. Was that a garden at the rear of the property? She couldn't tell for sure, but beyond the area there seemed to be nothing but dense woods.

"Elizabeth had a small parlor off the bedroom," Van said from somewhere behind her. His voice sounded hushed, as if he hated intruding on Ariele's contemplation of the yard.

She turned away from the window and followed Van through an archway into the parlor. Like the bedroom, it too was sparsely furnished. A desk and chair presided over one side of the small room; a huge wooden trunk occupied the opposite side. A lamp on a pole stood in between.

Ariele's attention immediately focused on the trunk. It looked ancient and battered, as if it had been well used. What did it hold? Bending down, she tried the latch, but it wouldn't budge.

"I see you're fascinated by old trunks."

Ariele peered up at Van. "Would you happen to know where the key to this one is?"

"No. But there are a few keys on a ring stashed in Elizabeth's safety-deposit box. I'll bet one of them will fit the lock on the trunk."

Ariele started to get up, but something

made her pitch forward, and she lost her balance. She reached out for the trunk in an attempt to keep from falling. Van got to her first. His hands grasped her arms, holding her tight.

"Are you okay?" he asked.

His breath warmed her cheek. It was a moment before she could answer, before she realized what had caused her near fall. One foot was numb. She shook it; a tingling sensation shot through her toes. "My foot went to sleep," she said, feeling slightly foolish.

Van looked amused, but his hands still held her, and Ariele gradually became aware of another sensation, one that made her even more uncomfortable. She felt off balance again, but for a very different reason. It had been years since she'd responded that way to a man's touch. And the man had been Jerod.

Flustered and confused, she broke free from Van, mumbling, "I'm fine now." She turned so that he couldn't see her face, setting her gaze on a picture, a photograph, that hung on the wall above the trunk. The picture was dim, but as Ariele examined it more closely, what she saw made her draw in a sharp breath. Her embarrassment over the little incident with Van fled her mind and she stared, transfixed, at the photograph of Elizabeth Sheldrake as a young woman.

It wasn't until Van spoke that Ariele realized he was looking at the photograph too. "Beautiful, wasn't she? Like you," he added quietly.

Ariele couldn't respond; she didn't know what to say. His words, "Beautiful . . . like you," echoed in her mind. But it wasn't the only reason she didn't answer him.

"You see it, don't you?" he said. "The hair, the eyes. The mouth, the nose."

The hair. Yes. In the picture, Elizabeth had dark hair, long, curly. *Like mine,* Ariele thought. The eyes that seemed to stare luminously into Ariele's own. Dark too — like hers. The mouth that was too generous, the lips that were slightly pouty, the nose that was small and straight — all like hers.

"The resemblance is striking, don't you think, Ariele?"

She regarded Van. "You've seen this picture before." It wasn't a question; she knew he had, and perhaps that explained why he had gazed at her so intently earlier in his office. "It never occurred to me that I might resemble her."

"No one ever told you?"

Ariele shook her head. Touching the photograph, she said, "I guess it must have been Aunt Elizabeth's secret."

"I imagine so. Ariele . . ."

She blinked, and Van came into focus. "Yes?"

"It's about time for me to get back to the office."

It took a moment for his words to register. "I'm sorry. I didn't know it was so late."

"Don't apologize. I wish I could show you the rest of the house and the grounds."

For some silly reason she wished he could too. "It's okay, Van," she quickly assured him. But as she followed him out of the room, her thoughts returned to the portrait. An odd feeling crept over her, as if she'd just seen herself in a time-dulled mirror. And she was compelled to wonder if their uncanny resemblance to each other was the reason Elizabeth Sheldrake had left most of her worldly goods to a niece she had barely known.

Chapter Three

On their way to the kitchen, Van showed Ariele the dining room. It was enormous, but like some of the other rooms, it didn't have much in the way of furniture. Ariele saw a dining table with — she counted — eight chairs, and a sideboard and a china closet filled with assorted dishes and glassware.

"The dining room's awfully big, isn't it?" she said, glancing at Van. "That is, for one person to be eating alone." Ariele was still thinking of her aunt, of the photograph in the upstairs parlor.

Van flashed her a grin. "Maybe not so big if that person had some company. Sorry I can't stay."

Ariele's thoughts snapped back to the present. Did he think she wanted *his* company? He must have picked up on her reaction to him when he'd caught her with his hands and kept her from falling. He was aware then that she found him attractive. No doubt the knowledge served to inflate his ego. She was not about to give it a further boost.

"At least Blanche is getting a nice dining set," she said finally.

"You're wrong. Blanche's set is stashed away in the storage room. The table's wobbly and scratched, and one of the chairs has a leg missing."

Ariele couldn't help smiling at the news. "Do you suppose the Pilchard sisters enjoy mending things?"

Van chuckled. "We'd better head to the kitchen and tell Emma that her efforts in fixing up the guest room weren't futile, after all."

The kitchen was a surprise to Ariele. Unlike the rest of Sheldrake, it sported modern appliances and furnishings. Emma stood over an impressive-looking stainless-steel range, stirring something in a pot. The smell of beef roasting permeated the air.

The housekeeper must have heard them come in. She turned around. "Have you made up your mind about the room, Miss Harwood?"

Ariele attempted a cheerful smile. "Yes. I've decided to stay tonight." The words were out and she couldn't take them back.

Emma's expression showed neither pleasure nor displeasure. "It's settled then." She lifted the pot off the stove and carried it to the sink. "My quarters are right beside the kitchen," she said over her shoulder.

Had Ariele heard correctly? Of course it was logical that Emma should live there. "Have you been at Sheldrake a very long time?" She hoped the question might thaw the housekeeper a little.

"Going on thirty years now." Emma slowly drained the water off the contents of the pot. Steam rose in a thick cloud from the sink. She set the pot on the counter. "I'm used to getting every other weekend off to visit my sister in Utica." The statement sounded more like a challenge, and she fixed her unblinking gaze on Ariele.

"That's fine, Emma." The reassurance was automatic on Ariele's part, though her mind made a quick calculation. Today was Tuesday. "Will you be off this coming weekend, then?"

The housekeeper considered the question. "No. The one after."

"So, it looks like everything's settled."

The optimistic comment came from Van. His expression struck Ariele as a bit smug, and she was tempted to tell him that she'd agreed to stay only because Emma had gone to so much trouble with the guest room. But she couldn't say that in Emma's presence.

Van went over to the housekeeper. "Miss Harwood's had a tiring trip. I think she'd enjoy having her dinner in the parlor."

Though he hadn't bothered to consult her, Ariele was glad for his suggestion. Maybe he'd thought of her comment about eating alone.

"I can bring you a tray, Miss Harwood."

"I'd like that, Emma."

The housekeeper stared past Ariele. "Miss Sheldrake took her dinner in the parlor. Ate there most every night, until her last year, that is."

The way Emma said it, and her guarded expression, gave Ariele cause to wonder if the housekeeper too had observed the striking resemblance between the new mistress and the former one.

Emma had worked for Elizabeth Sheldrake a long while. No doubt her loyalties lay with her former employer. And no doubt she had seen the picture in the upstairs parlor, perhaps many times. She might even have it memorized.

"I'm sorry about my aunt's death," Ariele said to fill the silence. She suddenly wished she could ask Emma how Elizabeth Sheldrake had died, but something made her hold back. Maybe she feared the

housekeeper would be shocked by her ig-
norance.

"Yes, I'm sure we're all sorry," Emma
said curtly. She crossed to the other end of
the kitchen, opened a drawer, and started
rummaging in it.

Ariele glanced at Van. "Don't worry," he
said under his breath. "Everything will be
okay."

Before she could reply, he left her and
went to a window that was near the sink.
As he gazed out, Ariele couldn't help but
admire his profile, the firm line of his hips,
his legs so neatly encased in the leather
pants. "Where's Denton?" he said at last.

Emma stopped her rummaging. "He's
been in town all day, Mr. Caulfield. Told
me he was going to get supplies." She resumed her search.

Ariele was curious. "Denton?"

"He's the gardener," Van explained.

"Oh . . . yes." It had almost slipped
Ariele's mind that there was another em-
ployee at Sheldrake besides Emma. Would
Denton be as cool toward her as the
housekeeper was? "Maybe I could meet
him tomorrow," she said.

"He'll be around then," Emma volun-
teered.

Van checked his watch. "I'll help you

with your luggage on my way out."

"That's not necessary," Ariele said quickly. "I only have two suitcases."

"I'll take care of them."

It was Emma again. Ariele turned and found herself facing the housekeeper. Emma had a long carving knife in her hand. It must have been what she was scarching for.

Ariele's eyes went to the serrated blade of the knife. "What I mean," Emma went on, "is that I'll take the cases upstairs and unpack them for you." She flipped the knife over in her hands and ran a finger down the entire length of the blade.

The gesture was an innocent one, Ariele knew. But for some reason it sent an edgy tingle up her back. Was it because she was more uneasy about spending the night in this rambling old house than she cared to admit? She tried to push the troublesome question away. Raising her eyes to Emma's, she said, "I'll leave my luggage at the bottom of the steps for you."

"That'll do," Emma replied. She started off, then stopped. "Miss Sheldrake requested her dinner be served promptly at six, Miss Harwood. Is that what you wish too?"

"Six is fine."

Emma went back to her task, and Ariele decided to accompany Van outside. She could use some fresh air.

But the day had turned sultry and still, and there was no breeze. Ariele cast an anxious glance at the sky. Some high puffy clouds were visible above the treetops, but they didn't look threatening.

"It could storm tonight," Van predicted, as if he'd read her mind. After a pause, he said, "Are you sure you'll be okay here tonight, Ariele?"

She looked at him, incredulous. "Isn't it kind of late to be asking me that?"

"You're probably right."

Neither of them spoke again until they reached their vehicles. At her car, Ariele got her purse and located her keys. She singled out the one that fit the trunk. Unexpectedly, Van stole the keys from her hands, opened the trunk, and retrieved the suitcases. "There," he said, returning her keys along with her luggage.

"Thank you . . . I suppose," she said, unable to hide her smile.

He smiled back. "My pleasure. Would you be able to come to my office around ten tomorrow morning? I'll have the papers ready for you to sign. Then together we'll go to the bank where Elizabeth kept her deposit box."

"Ten is fine."

He seemed to find her response humorous. His smile widened into a grin. "Are you always so agreeable when it comes to time, Ariele?"

She was tempted to tell Van that he was perilously close to testing the limits of her agreeableness. But she doubted that it would faze him. "I'll see you tomorrow," she said, ignoring his remark.

Aware that his eyes were on her, Ariele turned and started toward the manor. The last she heard from Van was his impatient gunning of The Litigator, followed by an earth-shaking roar that told her he was headed down the lane, away from Sheldrake.

Whatever her reservations about Emma, Ariele couldn't deny that the housekeeper was a terrific cook. The roast beef and Yorkshire pudding were delicious. For dessert Emma had made a berry cobbler, which she had served warm with a scoop of vanilla ice cream on top.

When Emma came to the parlor to take the empty tray, Ariele complimented her on the meal. "Glad you liked it, Miss Harwood," the housekeeper said. She hesitated. "Is there anything else you need?" Without waiting for an answer, she went on, "I've put away your clothes in the closet and chest of drawers upstairs."

"Thank you, Emma. I can't think of anything else right now."

Emma stayed put, her hands clasped together in front of her. "What time do you want your breakfast?"

As full as she was, Ariele found it difficult to plan ahead to the next meal. "I . . ." She didn't want to appear uncertain. "Nine o'clock. I'll be going into Larkspur in the morning."

The housekeeper looked thoughtful. "I see. Would you like to eat in the parlor or shall I bring a tray to your room?"

"You don't need to go to that bother."

A slight smile crossed Emma's lips. "No bother at all. I'll deliver it to your room in the morning." She made a little move, as if she would go. But instead she remained stubbornly in place.

Ariele cast about for something to say. She noted the manner in which the sun shone through the double glass doors. It fell across the floor, bathing the sofa and love seat in a sort of golden glow. "This is a cozy room," she commented.

"It was Miss Sheldrake's favorite," the housekeeper replied quietly. "As I told you before, she ate her dinner here almost every day." Emma paused. "I hope you get a good night's sleep, Miss Harwood," she added. Then she finally left the room.

Ariele stared after her. She wondered if she and Emma would come to feel more at ease with each other during her short stay here. She told herself it didn't matter whether the housekeeper kept her stiffly formal attitude. But a part of her hoped to forge a bit friendlier relationship with Emma.

Rising from the love seat, Ariele went over to the glass doors and stared out. The yard looked inviting. Though she had intended on retreating to the library after dinner, she decided that she would rather explore some of the grounds outside. The exercise should help her to rest better.

She went upstairs to the guest room to change her clothes. She found her clothes hung up, just as Emma had said. Her jeans and knit tops and dresses were all neatly arranged. For once, she was glad she had the tendency to overpack for a trip.

She quickly got out of her high heels and suit and put on a pair of jeans and her blue knit top. Coming from the guest room, Ariele automatically glanced down the hall toward the suite. To her surprise, the door to the suite was ajar. Hadn't Van shut it earlier? She decided to close it herself.

At the door, she paused. Had something moved inside the bedroom? Cautiously Ariele stepped into the room, expecting to find Emma there. She saw no sign of the housekeeper, but the drapes at one of the windows were billowing slightly. Then she noticed that the window was standing open. Someone had definitely been in the room after she and Van had left. Had Emma concluded the suite needed a good airing out in preparation for the new mistress?

Ariele's eyes moved to the bed. The dust ruffle of the spread swayed in the breeze; long shadows stretched over the bed. The satin material gleamed in the soft light. Elizabeth Sheldrake had slept there. *Now,* Ariele thought, *I'm expected to sleep here too.* The idea made her shiver, and she turned away.

Her gaze wandered across the room to the dressing table, and she went to investigate. A small chair matching the table was set against the wall nearby. Ariele pulled it around so that she could sit in front of the dressing table.

A number of perfume vials took up most of the table's surface. But Ariele's attention was more drawn to the brush and comb set that occupied a silver tray in the midst of the clutter. Picking up the set, she examined it. The brush and comb were clean, as though they'd recently been washed. No hairs were embedded in the fine bristles of the brush. *No dark curly hairs — like mine,* Ariele thought.

She laid aside the brush and comb and studied the array of vials. They came in a rainbow of colors — green, amber, pink, blue. Only one, a blue vial, appeared to have perfume in it. Ariele picked up the bottle and took out the stopper. The smell of roses wafted out. Strange. The delicate scent was her favorite. Had her aunt loved it as well? Ariele dabbed a bit of the perfume on her wrists.

"Is there anything I can help you with?"

Ariele started at the unexpected sound of Emma's voice. She whirled around to find the housekeeper standing at the foot of the bed, watching her. How had Emma known she would be in the suite? "No, I . . ." She started to get up. In her haste, she nearly sent several vials crashing to the floor. *Get a grip,* she admonished herself. She had every right to be where she was. But the awkward feeling stayed with her.

"I came in to close the window," she explained to the housekeeper. "The sky looks like there might be rain tonight."

The housekeeper crossed over to the window and peered out. "When the air's full of moisture and the wind stirs late in the day like this, it's a sure sign of a storm." She walked to where Ariele stood. "Are you certain, Miss Harwood, that you wouldn't rather sleep in this room than in the guest room?"

It occurred to Ariele that Emma's features were set in a stubborn line; her lower jaw jutted out in a determined way. *She knows I don't want to stay here; that's why she's putting me on the spot.* "No," she assured Emma emphatically. "I've found the guest room to be very satisfactory."

Emma didn't move, but turned her attention to the dressing table. After a moment she said, "All of these used to be filled with perfume." She made a gesture that took in the collection of vials. "Jasmine. Gardenia. Lilac." She reached for an amber vial.

"Aunt Elizabeth must have loved wearing perfume." Would the comment draw out the housekeeper, prompt her to relate more details about her former mistress's life?

"She did love her perfume. Miss Sheldrake was very much a lady. Quite delicate . . . and beautiful." She lifted her eyes to meet Ariele's. The guarded expression slipped back into place. "But what am I talking about?" she said with a self-deprecating laugh. She fingered the vial for a moment, then set it down on the table. "If there's nothing else you need, Miss Harwood, I'll be going."

Ariele thought of something, though her mind was more on Emma's remarks about her aunt. "There is one favor. Will you put the lights on in the hallway when it gets dark? I'm going for a walk around the grounds before I go to bed."

Emma gazed at her evenly. "The lights in the upstairs hall are always on at night. But it'll be dark outside within the hour if the storm comes."

"I'll be going then. Thank you." Ariele sensed the housekeeper's vigilant gaze was following her.

Ariele was halfway down the hall when she realized she still had the perfume vial in her hand. She retraced her steps to the suite. But on entering the bedroom, she saw no sign of Emma. Where had she disappeared to so quickly? Had she gone into the parlor for some reason? Rather than investigate the housekeeper's whereabouts, Ariele swiftly set the vial on the dressing table and retreated from the room.

Once she was away from the house, Ariele began to relax. The wind moving through the trees brought with it a suggestion of coolness. She lifted her face to the breeze, letting it wick away the perspiration on her cheeks and brow. Looking up at the sky, she saw a bank of fluffy clouds. She was no longer fooled by their benign appearance. They signaled the coming storm.

About a third of the distance across the vast yard, Ariele came upon a stone footpath. She decided to see where it would take her. Flanking the path on either side were raised beds of flowers arranged in a visually pleasing manner. Ariele admired the bright blooms. It seemed Denton had a flair for his work.

But soon the flowers gave way to tall bushes and shrubs, and their unkempt appearance caused Ariele to retract her silent praise of the gardener. The way became almost junglelike. Ivy and brambles crept over the path in places, obscuring the stones.

Disappointed by what she'd found, Ariele was about to turn back when she came to a fork that split the path into two trails. Neither trail looked particularly inviting, but inquisitiveness got the better of her and so she took off down one of them.

The trail led Ariele to a building. Drawing close, she realized that the small, forlorn-looking structure was a house. Or more accurately, it was a cottage. The gardener's cottage, she guessed.

Tangles of dark green ivy covered much of the cottage, which itself was dingy gray. It must have been attractive once upon a time. But, like so much of the estate, it had obviously fallen into neglect.

The windows were dark, lending an unsettling, eerie appearance to the cottage. Did the gardener enjoy living in such isolated surroundings? The blank windows tempted Ariele to peer in. She fought the urge. According to Emma, the gardener wasn't at home. But what if he suddenly returned? How might he feel if he caught the new mistress in the act of snooping around his home? She had enough difficulty coping with Emma's distrust of her. She didn't need to make an enemy of the gardener.

Reluctantly Ariele turned away and followed the trail back to where it merged with the other one. Looking skyward, she noted the clouds had lowered. Though the rain was sure to come soon, she surmised she might have enough daylight left to explore a little way along the other trail.

Her decision led to an unexpected — and intriguing — discovery. The trail, which started out narrow and twisted, opened up at last into what appeared to be the decaying remnants of a formal garden. It must be the garden she'd glimpsed from the window of the mistress's suite. A rose arbor burdened with crimson blooms formed a natural entrance to the garden.

Beside the arbor, a crumbling concrete bench offered a place of respite. Ariele cautiously tested out the bench. It held her without breaking apart. She could easily imagine her aunt sitting on the bench as a young woman. But had she been alone? Or had someone kept her company — a young man, to be specific? Had Elizabeth Sheldrake ever been in love? Even now, the bench and arbor made an undeniably romantic setting.

She'd been at the estate only a matter of hours and already she was full of questions about its former owner. Would she ever find the answers to them? She wasn't very hopeful.

Ariele reached out to pluck a rose from the arbor. In her attempt to break off the bloom, a thorn jagged her thumb and drew a bright bead of blood. She brushed the drop of blood away and got up from the bench.

At that moment her ears picked up the first rumbling volley of thunder. Echoing around the distant hills like cannon fire, it served as a warning to Ariele, not only of the nearness of the impending storm, but of the danger inherent in letting her mind wander too much.

Moving past the arbor, Ariele saw that the trail came to an abrupt end at the end of a thicket. Beyond the thicket, as far as she could tell, there was nothing but woods.

It seemed she had no other choice but to start back to the manor when she snatched a glimpse of something unusual in the thicket. She stopped and looked. The object appeared to be the head of an animal, perhaps a horse. Was it the remnant of another statue?

She stepped closer in order to get a better look, but she could barely see through the dense tangle of trees and undergrowth. Without warning, lightning slashed across the sky; it was followed by a loud snarl of thunder.

Ariele jumped, startled by more than the violent weather. In the next instant another streak of lightning lit up the thicket and she froze, her eyes riveted on what she saw there.

Chapter Four

Van's face registered surprise. "A merry-go-round? Are you *sure* that's what you saw?"

Ariele leaned forward in her chair. "Yes, I'm sure," she said quietly.

Though she couldn't blame Van for his skepticism, she knew what she had seen entangled in the thicket. And nothing he might say could change her mind on the matter. "I'm not mistaken."

"I believe you" was Van's only comment.

If he'd asked, she would have been glad to tell him the exact impression she'd had of the carousel in the instant when the lightning had flashed through the thicket. She would have said that its roof was partly caved in, that some of the horses were toppled over, but that others still stood upright on their wooden poles. And she would have confessed that she'd waited in a torrent of rain, hoping for one more glimpse of the incredible sight.

"Could you show me the carousel tomorrow?" Van's question drew her back.

This time Ariele met his gaze. She wondered what his thoughts were behind those impassive eyes. "Of course I'll show you."

Van gave his attention to the pile of papers stacked on his desk, the papers that she had just signed. He shuffled them and returned them to the folder from which he'd taken them earlier. Then he got up and came around the desk to stand beside her chair.

"I take it the storm didn't change your mind about staying at Sheldrake."

Annoyance rose in Ariele over his remark. Yet she had never been more acutely conscious of Van's nearness. Her eyes drifted from his face to his clothing. He wore a matching brown leather vest and pants. The crisp-looking cotton shirt underneath was in a shade of blue that matched his eyes. "I'm not afraid of storms, Van," she said defiantly.

"We were lucky last night, Ariele." His eyes crinkled with humor. "Around here the power usually gets knocked out at the first lightning strike. If it happens after dark, the problem doesn't get fixed until morning."

Was he baiting her now? She raised her chin a notch. "Then I'll be forced to use candles, won't I? Besides, it won't matter if the electricity goes out at night."

Van leaned close and smiled. "Candles can be very romantic under certain circumstances, you know."

"Yes," she murmured. Why were they flirting with each other this way? Ariele put most of the blame on Van, but she couldn't deny that she was enjoying the encounter.

Van laughed, as if he could read her thoughts. Then he went to the other side of the desk and took a manila envelope from one of the drawers. "Zelda and Blanche asked to pick up their inheritances tomorrow," he said, his professional demeanor slipping back into place. "If it's okay with you, I'll plan to bring the sisters out to the estate around one-thirty."

"It's okay." Ariele felt a measure of dread at the thought of seeing the sisters again. But with Van escorting them, how much trouble would they be able to cause? "Do they live nearby? That is, how will they transport the piano and the furniture?"

"To answer your first question, they live together in a drafty old house about the same size as Sheldrake in a burg called Darbyville. It's about twenty miles from here. As for how they're going to haul away the piano and table and chairs . . ." He shrugged. "Let's be glad it's not our problem. For now, why don't we concentrate on getting you to the Burroughs County Bank, where Elizabeth kept her deposit box. The key we'll need to open the box is in here." He held up the manila envelope.

Ariele debated over what she might find in the box as she accompanied Van down the hallway to the reception area of his office. She had never cared about wealth, never entertained the notion that she would one day come into a large inheritance. At the same time, she could certainly use any money her aunt might have chosen to leave her.

Van stopped at the receptionist's desk. Ariele noted that the receptionist looked no less glamorous now than she had the day before. Despite the fact that she had applied her makeup carefully that morning and combed her hair into a semblance of style, Ariele still felt frumpy by comparison.

The receptionist gazed up at Van. "Mr. Simms called. He won't be able to make it until three."

"I'm not surprised," Van replied. "Thanks, Darcy."

So Darcy was the receptionist's name. Ariele decided that it fit her. She watched as Van put his hand on the back of Darcy's chair. His fingers almost touched the long blond strands of Darcy's hair.

Ariele averted her eyes, but she heard Van say, "I'm taking Miss Harwood to the bank now. I should be back in half an hour, in plenty of time for lunch." The way he put it made Ariele think that he and Darcy had a date for lunch. Glancing back, she caught the look that passed between the attorney and his receptionist, and she suspected that the two might have a personal relationship with each other, as well as a professional one.

All at once Ariele was upset with herself. No doubt Van viewed flirting as a form of amusement. He had to know that women found him attractive, and he didn't hesitate to take advantage of the situation.

By the time Van joined her, Ariele had worked herself into a minor stew. When he asked if she was ready, she replied crisply, "Whenever you are."

Van seemed oblivious to any change in her mood. "The bank's about a block away," he said, studying her high heels. "Do you want to walk or ride?"

By "ride" did he mean that motorcycle of his? "Are you kidding? Let's walk." She forged ahead of him out the door.

It wasn't until Ariele had gone by two

storefronts that she realized Van wasn't with her. She came to a slow stop and turned around.

Van stood on the sidewalk outside his office. He grinned and waved at her. "The bank's the other way," he called.

Ariele felt the absolute fool as she retraced her steps back to him. But he didn't make any further comment and they went along without talking for a few minutes.

Finally Van broke the silence. "These are all compliments of the Larkspur Historical Society," he said, pointing toward an island of benches and tubs of flowers. "The Society is very active around town," he added.

The lapse in conversation had given Ariele the chance to compose herself. "The society that Philip Hubbard is the president of."

"Yes." Van came to a halt. He turned to face her. "Philip Hubbard and the Larkspur Historical Society think Sheldrake would be an ideal site for their proposed museum."

"Really?" Ariele thought that Van looked uncharacteristically somber. "Then that's good news for me, isn't it?" she said, feeling him out.

Van regarded her. "There are plenty of

75

other possibilities for Sheldrake." He resumed walking again, at a quicker pace than before. Ariele had to hurry to keep up with his long strides. When they came to the bank, he paused on the steps that led up to the doors. "Your aunt never envisioned turning Sheldrake into a local exhibit. She wasn't a particular fan of Philip Hubbard, either."

"Why did she leave something to the Society?"

Van held the door for Ariele. "Elizabeth didn't say exactly. She did tell me that she once belonged to the Society herself, not so much as an active member, but more to help keep the group's coffers filled. I suppose she felt a certain sense of civic responsibility to remember them in her will."

Ariele accepted his explanation. But it left a few questions in her mind.

A short, middle-aged woman met them at the customer service desk. "I've been expecting you, Mr. Caulfield," she said briskly. "Please come with me."

The customer service representative led them to a vault near the back of the bank. The vault's walls were lined with deposit boxes. The representative took down a box from the far wall and brought it to a counter where Ariele and Van waited.

To her surprise, Ariele's palms began to perspire as she watched Van use the key from the manila envelope to open the box. The representative had him sign a piece of paper. "Let me know when you're finished," she said. Then she gave Ariele a smile and left the vault, closing the door behind her.

Van looked inquisitively at Ariele. "So . . ."

"So . . ." she repeated. Not only were her palms clammy, but her hands also began to tremble. "I guess this is the moment of truth, isn't it?"

"You won't be disappointed."

Hadn't she heard that before? Peering into the box, she saw there were just three items inside — a fat brown envelope, a large key ring with several keys on it, and a green cloth pouch tied with a white ribbon.

Ariele removed the pouch and undid the ribbon. When she turned the pouch upside down, two pins and a necklace fell out onto the counter. One of the pins was encrusted with tiny diamonds and pearls, she noted; the other was a cameo. "I believe these belong to Zelda and Blanche," she said, holding them up for Van's inspection.

"I believe you're right," he agreed.

Ariele set the pins aside and examined the necklace. It was fashioned of silver in the form of a simple chain with a heart-shaped locket attached. The initials "E.S." were etched on the front of the piece.

Opening the catch on the locket, Ariele discovered a tiny photograph inside. It was a picture of a man with thick, wavy blond hair. Though the photo was clouded by age, she could see that the man was very handsome. But who was he?

"What's captured your attention?"

"This." She showed Van the photograph. "Do you know who he is?"

Van shook his head. "I know who he isn't," he said after a moment. "He's not Samuel Sheldrake — that is, Elizabeth's father."

"A brother then?"

"No. Elizabeth's only brother died of pneumonia when he was six years old."

Ariele studied the faded photograph again. She thought of the rose arbor and the bench she'd come upon the evening before. She'd wondered if Elizabeth had sat on the bench alone. "Maybe Elizabeth was in love with him." She glanced up at Van.

"Could be," he said softly.

"She never said anything to you about . . ."

"Never." Van was silent a moment. "Why don't you ask Emma? She probably

78

knows more about Elizabeth than anyone else does."

Ariele cringed inside at the idea of quizzing Emma about her employer's love life. She wished there was another person who could tell her. "I guess I could ask her," she said finally. She snapped the locket shut and returned it to the pouch.

"Why don't you open this now?" Van handed her the brown envelope.

The envelope was secured with a red wax seal. Carefully Ariele loosened the seal and pried open the flap. She let out a soft cry at what she saw inside. The envelope was filled with money — all bills, she discovered as she pulled out handful after handful. They were in denominations of one hundred and five hundred dollars. No mere pocket change, she realized.

"They're all the same," Van commented. "And just to prepare you, when they're added up, they total twenty-five thousand dollars."

"Twenty-five thousand?" she said shakily.

"I see you're surprised again."

Ariele tried to laugh, but it sounded more like a nervous hiccup. "A little."

Van chuckled. "Elizabeth didn't particularly trust banks. She told me she'd never had a savings account, never bought a bond or a certificate of deposit."

"I'm sure that doesn't matter." Ariele had enough difficulty comprehending that the money she held in her hands was hers.

"I don't suppose you'll want to carry that around with you."

She gave Van a wan smile. "No . . . of course not." She stuffed the bills back into the envelope and returned the envelope to the deposit box. "I'll leave it here for safe-keeping. For now," she added.

"You'll need the key." Van handed her the one that he had used to open the box.

His mention of the key reminded Ariele of the several stashed in the deposit box. "I'd like to take these too," she said, indicating the ring with the keys on it.

She began to put the jewelry pouch away when she decided she wanted to take the locket with her as well. Then she thought of the pins. "Should I keep them for Zelda and Blanche since they'll be at the estate tomorrow?" she asked.

"Not unless you want to take responsibility for them. Those jewels are worth a lot of loot. Besides, I'm planning to bring the old . . . ah, *ladies* by the bank first."

Ariele caught the gleam in Van's eye. She laughed at his near slip of the tongue as she placed the pouch in the deposit box.

Their business concluded, they left the bank. Van started in the direction of his office. When Ariele didn't follow, he stopped. "Aren't you coming?" he asked her.

"No. I believe I'll do some window-shopping, see what Larkspur has to offer."

"More than you'd think," Van said with a smile. He reached in his pocket and drew out a small card. "I meant to give this to you yesterday." He scribbled something on the back of the card and handed it to Ariele. "My office and home phone numbers," he explained, "in case you ever need to reach me."

Ariele doubted that would be necessary, but she smiled and thanked him as she placed the card in her purse next to Philip Hubbard's. She stood for a moment, watching while Van walked away from her. It would have been easy to go with him. But what purpose would it serve? He already had plans to take his attractive receptionist to lunch. Deliberately she turned in the other direction.

The idea of lunch reminded Ariele that she was hungry, and she began to look for a restaurant among the quaint shops lining the sidewalk. She soon spotted a red-canopied café named Munday's.

Inside the café, she was seated by the

hostess at a booth near a window. A low hum of conversation drifted through the small restaurant, and Ariele observed that most of the tables and booths were occupied by men and women in business attire. She guessed Munday's must be a favorite with the downtown lunch crowd. Were Van and Darcy part of that crowd?

A plump but pretty waitress dropped off a menu and a glass of ice water. Perusing the menu, Ariele chose the perch platter. The waitress efficiently took her order and hurried off toward the rear of the café.

Ariele settled back against the booth and picked up the glass of water. She was about to take a sip when she heard a decidedly masculine voice say, "What a wonderful coincidence this is."

Her recognition of the voice nearly caused Ariele to drop the glass. Instinctively she knew the words were meant for her, and her heart gave a sickening thud. Looking up, she met the brooding eyes of the man who had spoken.

"I have to apologize, Miss Harwood. I'm afraid I wasn't the gentleman yesterday that I usually am." The man named Archer smiled down at her — a blatantly conceited smile, she noted. He wore shorts again and a polo shirt, both in a dazzling

82

shade of white. He looked like he'd just come from a set of tennis.

"Of course," he went on, "I'd have to say that Van wasn't much of a gentleman either, since he failed to introduce us. But that's not surprising. He doesn't exactly have a sterling reputation around town in that regard." He offered Ariele his hand. "I'm Archer Winslow, and it's my pleasure to meet you."

Ariele ignored the gesture. "How did you know my name, Mr. Winslow?"

Archer Winslow dropped his hand, but not his smile. He took a step closer to the booth. "I make it a point to get acquainted with my neighbors," he said smoothly.

Ariele sat very still. "Neighbors?"

He laughed softly. "Oh, of course. It figures that Van didn't tell you that either. I own Winslow Farms. My property borders Sheldrake to the south."

"I see, Mr. Winslow," she said with thinly disguised politeness.

Bending over the booth, he rested his arm on the back. "Just Archer."

Ariele's response was a chilly smile. Mr. Winslow seemed to take a lot for granted. One, that she found him irresistibly attractive. "Well, it was nice to meet you." Would he take the hint and go?

Archer Winslow leaned closer. "Would you mind if I joined you for a few minutes, Miss Harwood? I'm waiting for a friend, and he's always late."

Before Ariele could reply that she'd rather eat alone, he eased into the booth on the opposite side. How crass could the man be?

He lifted his hand in a signal to the waitress. She came on the run. "Mr. Winslow!" she said breathlessly. "I wasn't expecting you this early."

"Marilee, you should know by now how unpredictable I can be." His hand brushed against hers.

Marilee giggled; her cheeks flushed pink. "Do you know what you want, Mr. Winslow?"

"I know exactly what I want, Marilee, but I hardly think that's a topic for discussion at the moment." His eyes were glued on Ariele.

Ariele squirmed and glanced away. Her fingers worried at the edges of her napkin. Was it intuition that warned her Archer Winslow was not only crass, but possibly dangerous as well? Vaguely she heard him order a glass of iced tea.

"Now, where were we?"

Ariele forced herself to look at him. "I

believe you had just invited yourself to sit down, Mr. Winslow."

"I love it! Your sense of humor, that is, Miss Harwood." His eyes held hers. "And your spirit. I find it very stimulating." His tea came and he took a sip before he spoke again. "I realize that you don't know me, so let me tell you a little about myself. I raise and breed racehorses. It's a profitable business, and I'm undeniably proud of my farm." He paused. "I hope you'll allow me to take you on a tour. I think you'll be most impressed."

If the invitation had come from anyone else, she might have accepted it. But her suspicion of Archer Winslow caused her to hedge. "I doubt I can find the time since I won't be in Larkspur long."

"What a shame." He reached in his shirt pocket and drew out a card, which he handed to her. "I'll be available any time during the next few days. Call me, and I'll personally escort you through my stable barns."

Ariele looked at the card. It seemed she was in the business of collecting them lately. "Thank you, but don't count on it."

"Well then, perhaps I should get right to the point."

"The point?"

He rested his elbows on the table and steepled his lean, brown hands together. The opposing tips of his fingers and thumbs lightly touched each other. "I understand you've inherited Sheldrake, and I want to buy it from you." When she didn't reply, he laughed. "Your ears didn't fool you, Miss Harwood. I want to buy your property, and I don't mind admitting that I'm determined about the matter."

Here, suddenly, she was being presented with the opportunity to get rid of her inheritance. Then why was she hesitating? For some reason, her tongue couldn't form the words she should say. What came out of her mouth instead was a garbled "You do . . . That is, you're sure that you . . ."

Ariele got no further. From the corner of her eye she caught sight of a flash of red hair, and her attention was drawn across the room. There, heading in her direction, was Van with his receptionist in tow.

Was it only Ariele's imagination or were Van's eyes set on her? Not just on her, she saw when he came closer. They were darting back and forth between herself and Archer Winslow, and she could all but feel the heat of Van's anger even before he came to a halt at their booth. Darcy hung back, behind Van, as if she sensed something unpleasant was about to happen.

No one said anything for a charged moment. Archer Winslow finally broke the silence. "Van, what a surprise to see —"

"What are you doing here?" Van cut in.

Archer smiled wryly. "Besides the fact that it's none of your business, I think the answer is obvious. I was just being neighborly." He lowered his hands to the table and took a minute to examine his fingernails. Then he fixed Van with a hard stare. "It's something of a habit with me." His gaze shifted to Ariele. "Having lunch at Munday's, that is."

The animosity that hung in the air between the two men was almost palpable. And the looks they exchanged held plenty of meaning too. They told Ariele that Van and Archer had a deep-seated hatred for each other. She wondered what had caused it.

"You know what I'm driving at," Van said at last.

"Yes, and it'll do you little good."

Another silence followed, and Ariele sensed that Van was watching her. She looked at him. Those blue eyes spoke volumes to her — if only she could read them.

The next instant Archer rose from the

booth. "On the other hand, if you two have a date for lunch, I certainly have no intention of interfering. Not for a moment," he added in a way that implied it was the very thing he would have done. He turned to Ariele. "I'll be in touch soon. That's a promise."

Then Archer turned away, and Ariele was left to face Van. The attorney stared at her grimly, but that didn't deter her from what she had to say. "Van Caulfield, you owe me an explanation."

"Gladly," he retorted, but no explanation was forthcoming.

Just then Marilee appeared, bearing the perch platter. Van stepped aside, and she set the platter on the table in front of Ariele. "Will there be anything else?" she asked with a chipper smile.

Ariele regarded her meal glumly. "No, nothing else." The smell of the broiled fish made her suddenly nauseous.

The waitress departed, and Van started to go too. Darcy followed after him, her head lowered. Ariele couldn't blame the receptionist, and she felt a twinge of sympathy for the young woman.

When he'd gone a couple of steps, Van stopped. Glancing back, he said, "Tomorrow we'll talk, Ariele." Then he strode off.

Ariele pushed the platter aside. She should eat, but she couldn't. Her stomach would have to stay empty for now. But her mind was filled with questions. At the moment there was one that she particularly wanted an answer to. Sheer masculine appeal aside, how could Darcy work for such an impetuous, fiery-tempered attorney, let alone date him?

Chapter Five

Ariele spent the afternoon ensconced in the library at Sheldrake. After the way her morning had gone, she desperately needed some peace and quiet. Her intention was to start inventorying the titles in the collection. But between attempting to make sense of the charged scene between Van and Archer Winslow, and fighting back the most ridiculous little surge of jealousy over Van's apparent relationship with Darcy, she accomplished a lot less than she would have liked to.

With a sigh, Ariele took stock of the books she had arranged in piles around her. Of the fifty or so titles she'd perused, she had happened upon a few that were virtual treasures — a thick, leather-bound anthology of Tennyson's poems; a collection of short stories by Dickens; another by Goethe. But her excitement over the discoveries was blunted by her other concerns, and with a certain weariness she looked for a spot to set the books aside for consideration later.

A table nearby displayed a glass vase and an alabaster bust of a young girl. It would do, she decided. She removed the vase and bust and set the books in their place. She'd just finished the task when Emma appeared in the doorway, bearing a tray in her hands.

"I thought you might like some lemonade and cookies," the housekeeper said.

After her upset at lunch, Ariele hadn't thought about food. But now the mention of cookies made her hungry. "I'd love some, Emma."

The housekeeper carried the tray over to the table. "The cookies just came out of the oven." She laid the tray beside the books.

Ariele took a cookie from the tray and ate a bite of it. The cookie was chocolate chip, and it was gooey and delicious. "Mmm. Wonderful."

Emma beamed. Then she noticed the books on the table and those piled on the floor. "Miss Sheldrake had the greatest respect for literature. But I'm sure you can see that from her collection." Emma ran a callused finger along the spine of the Tennyson volume.

Ariele took advantage of the remark to gain a common ground with the housekeeper. "I love books too. In fact, I'm a librarian."

Emma's eyebrows shot up. "Are you? Miss Sheldrake would have been happy to hear that."

Smiling, Ariele told the housekeeper, "I wish that I could keep all the books in this library."

Emma looked surprised. "Why can't you?"

Chagrined, Ariele knew that she'd said too much. But she didn't feel ready yet to tell Emma that she planned to sell the estate. "Maybe I will be able to keep them." She searched for another topic of conversation and suddenly remembered the locket in her purse. "Emma, I came upon something in my aunt's safety-deposit box that intrigued me."

When she saw that she had Emma's interest, she got the necklace from her purse. "I was wondering if you had ever seen this before." She handed the closed locket to the housekeeper.

Emma examined it, turning it over in her hands. "Yes, I remember it. Miss Sheldrake wore this necklace almost every day of her life."

Ariele took back the locket and opened it. "There's a picture of a man inside. Do you know him?" She showed Emma.

Emma's expression changed. Her mouth tightened into a thin line; her brow furrowed, as if all at once she were worried about something. When she gave no answer, Ariele persisted. "Can you tell me about him? I thought he might be Samuel Sheldrake." She knew very well that he wasn't from what Van had said, but she was anxious to hear Emma's response.

The housekeeper shook her head. She snapped the locket shut in Ariele's hand. "I can't tell you who it is. I'm sorry." She began to back away. "If you'll excuse me, Miss Harwood, I've got work to do."

Ariele was painfully aware that Emma had lied to her, that the housekeeper knew something — perhaps much — about the man in the photograph. But she sensed it would do no good to pressure the housekeeper. If she were patient, she might find another opportunity to broach the subject.

The housekeeper headed for the door. She paused just long enough to ask Ariele if she'd like her dinner in the parlor again.

"Yes, thank you, Emma," she replied automatically.

After Emma had gone, Ariele picked up the cookie and absently nibbled on it. Around her the manor was quiet, almost unnaturally so. The only sound her ears detected was the faint ticking of a clock somewhere. It couldn't be the mantel clock; that timepiece, she'd noticed, didn't make any sound.

Her mind wasn't on clocks, however. It was fixed on the handsome image of the man in the locket, and what that man had meant to the woman who'd faithfully worn his picture close to her breast for many years. Why had Emma refused to tell her anything about him? Was it because he'd been a rogue who had shamelessly captured, then broken, Elizabeth Sheldrake's heart?

Another image insinuated itself into her mind — the portrait of her aunt that hung in the upstairs parlor. Was Emma reminded of her former mistress every time she looked into the new mistress's face?

And what about the carousel? How might the housekeeper respond if she learned that the new mistress had discovered it? Ariele sighed. If only her aunt were alive! She would divulge the secrets of Sheldrake to her inquisitive niece. Wouldn't she?

As she was eating dinner, Ariele thought of the trunk and of the keys on the ring in her purse. Van had said one of those keys would likely fit the trunk. If she could get the trunk open, she might discover a clue that could help her identify the man in the locket.

The temptation was great to rush upstairs and find out. But she was bone tired, and there were the books in the library that she should return to their respective shelves. She decided to put off an investigation of the trunk until morning.

Besides, the pale stream of sunlight that came through the double glass doors told her that it would be night soon. A check of her watch confirmed the fact. It was nearly eight-thirty.

Ariele paused at the doors to admire the view of the sky. A few high clouds were swirled with deepening shades of lavender and pink, reflections of the setting sun. It seemed the weather would be fair tonight, and that seemed a good sign, at least.

In contrast to the brightness of the sky, the lawn of the manor lay cloaked in long shadows that stretched away into blackness at the fringes of the grass. For some reason the scene reminded Ariele of the gardener's isolated, ivy-shrouded cottage and of the old formal garden with the headless statue of Pan and the carousel hidden in the thicket. Maybe it was because the images provoked in her a feeling of sadness that she felt suddenly chilly. Turning away from the doors, she went into the library.

Ariele immediately set to work reshelving the books. When the task was finished, she picked up the three volumes she'd laid aside and returned the vase and sculpture to their proper places on the table.

Holding the books against her, she stepped through the sliding door and back into the parlor. Just as she was about to cross the room, something caught her eye — a slight movement, more like a flicker — from near the doorway that led into the hall. Ariele stopped in her tracks, and the flicker became a shadow. "Emma?" she called out tentatively.

No response came, and she strained to see whether she had only imagined someone was there. She knew it wasn't her imagination when the shadow moved toward her, taking the shape of a man. For a moment Ariele was confused. Then she guessed who he was. "You must be Denton."

He came closer. "Yes."

His voice was low, gravelly, as if he had a cold. In the dearth of light, Ariele couldn't see his face plainly or determine his age, though he couldn't be old. He was a large man, big-boned. Hulking was a word that came to Ariele's mind. She took a step backward. "I'm Ariele Harwood, Elizabeth Sheldrake's great-niece."

Denton stood near a lamp, yet he didn't move to turn it on. "I know," he said. "Welcome to Sheldrake."

The welcome sounded anything but cordial. "Thank you," she said at last, looking at him uncertainly. Why had he come into the parlor? To fill the silence, she said, "I understand you live in a cottage on the grounds." She didn't volunteer that she'd seen his home and been tempted to peek in its windows.

"That's right."

Denton turned slightly so that she got a glimpse of his features. He had a prominent nose and light-colored hair that fell down over his forehead in an unkempt manner. Though his eyes were hidden from her in the growing darkness, she could feel them observing her. Gathering her courage, she asked, "What are you doing in the manor?"

He held up his other hand to reveal a small package. "I was in the kitchen."

For a moment Ariele was puzzled. "You mean Emma gave you something to eat."

"Yes."

Ariele began to wonder if Denton might be shy. That would explain his terse answers, the reticence on his part. But it didn't explain the slight qualm she felt in his presence.

He started away from her. "I'd better be going," he said, turning toward the glass doors.

Ariele told herself that he'd just been uncomfortable in her presence. Perhaps it was to be expected. She thought of something to say that might put him at ease. "Denton," she called after him. "I wanted to tell you that you've done a nice job on the front lawn."

"Thanks," was his only response. Then he went out, pulling the door shut behind him.

Ariele looked after him until he rounded the corner of the manor. Setting her books aside, she checked the double doors. Both were unlocked. Didn't Emma bother to secure them in the evenings? Or were they left open all night? The notion that the gardener could wander in and out of them at will gave Ariele the shivers. She tinkered with the latches until she got them bolted. Testing the doors, she found she couldn't budge them — and that's the way she was determined they would stay.

Chapter Six

The next morning Ariele wakened to sun-shine streaming through the windows of the guest room. She knew at once that she had overslept. Consulting her watch, she saw the time was nine-thirty. She was used to rising early. Even during the summer months, when her work schedule was curtailed, she never got up later than seven. Now, despite having spent a good ten hours in bed, she felt groggy. It was little wonder. The night before she'd had a lot of trouble settling down to sleep.

She'd reasoned that a large part of the blame could be put on her new surround-ings and the fact that she was beginning to emerge from the slight daze she'd been in since learning she was an heiress. But something else had contributed to her rest-lessness, and she traced it to a sense of dis-quiet that had come over her after her encounter with the gardener.

In the rational light of day, she knew she'd blown the little scene in the parlor out of proportion. Maybe Denton was a bit creepy, like the cottage he lived in. But there was nothing more to it than that. He was certainly no threat to her well-being.

If she wanted to lose sleep over someone whose actions she might perceive as threatening, she'd be better off to consider Archer Winslow. Now that she thought of it, couldn't her sleepless state have been more due to her upset over Archer's intrusion on her privacy at the café — not to mention the brief altercation he'd had with Van — than to any actions on Denton's part?

With a sigh, Ariele swung her legs over the side of the bed and got up. She had a busy day ahead of her whether she was tired or not. After breakfast she would get started on the trunk in the upstairs parlor. Then she had Van and the Pilchard sisters to look forward to in the afternoon.

Ariele found her breakfast waiting on a tray on top of the chest of drawers. Emma had obviously delivered it, while having the courtesy not to waken the new mistress from her sleep. Ariele ate the cereal and fruit on the tray. She set the empty tray in the corridor in case the housekeeper should return, then headed off to the bathroom for a quick bath.

She had just slipped into a pair of jeans when she heard a soft knock at the door.

Emma's voice called out, "Miss Harwood? Are you up?"

Hurriedly Ariele fastened the jeans. "Just a minute." She yanked a blouse from its hanger and shrugged into it on her way to the door. "What is it, Emma?" she asked, opening to the housekeeper.

Emma appeared perplexed. "I'm sorry to bother you, but Misses Zelda and Blanche Pilchard are downstairs."

Ariele's mouth fell open. "Zelda and . . ."

The housekeeper smiled nervously. "It's true, I'm afraid. They're in the parlor, and they want to see you."

"But . . . They were supposed to come with Va . . . Mr. Caulfield this afternoon."

"Perhaps they misunderstood," Emma offered, though she sounded skeptical. "Older people get confused sometimes."

Confused, nothing! thought Ariele. The sisters were as sharp as hawks circling their prey. But it might not be wise to argue the point with the housekeeper.

"Shall I tell them you'll be down?"

There seemed no choice. "Of course, Emma."

As soon as the housekeeper left, Ariele went to her purse and got out Van's business card. Whatever it was the Pilchard sisters were up to, she was sure the attorney would want to know about it.

Ariele picked up the phone, but when she held the receiver to her ear, there was no dial tone. The line was dead. "That's strange," she muttered to herself. She placed the receiver in its cradle, then lifted it again. Still no sound. She dialed anyway, but her efforts proved futile.

Ariele inspected the cord that led from the phone. She pulled the table out from the wall and looked to see if the cord could have worked loose from the wall socket. It hadn't. She jiggled the cord, wondering if the problem might be a short in the wire. But a check of the phone showed that wasn't it either. Finally she gave up and went downstairs to face Zelda and Blanche.

She found them sitting side by side on the sofa in the parlor. They were dressed in identical baggy beige pants and plaid long-sleeved shirts in warring shades of red and green. On their heads they wore huge straw hats whose brims effectively hid their mops of hair and shielded their prying eyes. But Ariele had no doubt those eyes were observing her critically as she crossed the room.

It was after she came to a stop in front of the sisters that she noticed their mammoth handbags. The bags, which were propped on either side of Zelda and Blanche, more closely resembled overnight cases than purses. They sported lavish displays of sequins and rhinestones. Were the designs the sisters' handiwork? Ariele had a sudden wicked urge to dump the purses upside down and expose their contents.

Zelda sniffed, and Ariele's thoughts turned from the bags to the woman who owned one of them. Determined not to be intimidated by the tall sister, she asked, "Why are you here? I wasn't expecting you until this afternoon when Mr. Caulfield was to come with you."

Zelda sprang from the sofa. "What did I tell you, Blanche?" She peered down her nose at Ariele. "Mr. Caulfield didn't telephone you about our change in plans, Miss Harwood?"

"Change?"

The word was barely out of Ariele's mouth before Zelda broke in. "That young man is highly irresponsible! We gave him explicit instructions to inform you that we would not be able to come at the arranged time, that you were to receive us this morning instead." She turned to her sister. "You see, Blanche, he's incapable of honoring the simplest request!" Her head pivoted back to Ariele. "I must tell you, Miss Harwood, that Blanche and I will not be inconvenienced waiting for some boorish, blundering lawyer to follow through on his messages." Her chin jutted stubbornly.

The stout sister hefted herself up. "You were right, Zelda," she said with a certain smugness. "As you almost always are, I might add." She beamed at her sister, then set snapping eyes on Ariele.

The skin at the back of Ariele's neck prickled at the rancorous attack. She had a fierce desire to rise to Van's defense, to tell the self-righteous Pilchard sisters that there was nothing blundering or boorish about Cyril Vance Caulfield III, that he could hardly be expected to inform her of anything when her phone wasn't in working order. But she strongly suspected that the sisters would conclude she was making up lies to protect the attorney. So all she said was, "I'm sure that some urgent matter must have kept Mr. Caulfield from phoning me."

Zelda snorted. "Ha! I would have expected you to say that. And I'm certain that young Mr. Caulfield in his tight pants has made fools of women far more knowledgeable in the ways of the world than *you,* Miss Harwood." She snatched up her handbag and put her back to Ariele. "Come along," she ordered her sister. "Let's get on with it."

"Yes, let's do," Blanche enthused.

Both infuriated and stung by Zelda's insinuations, Ariele stood for a moment, unable to ask just what it was they planned to get on with. She watched with some detachment as the sisters made a beeline for the piano.

"Miss Harwood." Zelda's harping voice rang out, bringing Ariele to attention. "I wish to say I've no intention of taking this instrument with me."

"Why not?" Ariele responded in a rare cutting tone. "The piano's yours."

Zelda's mouth curled in a contemptuous smile. "Thank you for stating the obvious. But I don't want it, so I'm giving it to you, Miss Harwood. You see, I've never been musically inclined. You, though —" she directed a bony finger in Ariele's direction — "You're still young. If you haven't already learned to play the piano, it's not too late."

"The piano is such a lovely instrument," Blanche said with a sigh. "I regret I have no musical talent, either." She ran a hand across the closed keyboard.

Ariele watched with distaste as Blanche's fat fingers left smudges on the shiny surface. A thought occurred to her. Was either sister aware that the piano played songs by itself? She chose not to tell them.

Zelda shook her head. "Poor dear Elizabeth. She should have known better than to leave it to one of us. But she was so very . . . in such a *confused* state of mind at the last." She shoved back the brim of her hat so that her eyes were fully visible to Ariele.

Those eyes held scorn; was it only for her? Ariele wondered. Or was it for Elizabeth Sheldrake too? And what did Zelda mean by "confused state of mind"?

Zelda averted her gaze. "I hope you'll receive much enjoyment from the piano, Miss Harwood," she said in an oddly quiet voice.

"Thank you, but I'd like to consult with Mr. Caulfield before I accept your offer."

Zelda rounded on her. "Mr. Caulfield!" She spat out the name. "What agreements you and I might come to are none of his affairs." Just as rapidly her mood seemed to shift again from threatening to benevolent. "Forgive me for not understanding your reluctance. I do now, and I have the ideal solution. Come with me."

Before Ariele could protest, Zelda headed off at a trot toward the hall. By the time Ariele caught up with her, Zelda had gone nearly the length of the hallway. She came to a stop in front of a closed door.

"Here we are," she exclaimed.

Ariele realized that in her haste she hadn't kept track of Blanche. A nervous glance around showed no sign of the stout sister. "Where's Blanche?" she demanded of Zelda.

But Zelda was fumbling with the doorknob. After a moment she said over her shoulder, "You mustn't worry about Blanche. She's perfectly capable of taking care of herself. Besides, she knows every nook and cranny of the manor. And she *adores* going off on her own. Ah! There, I've got it." Zelda gave the door a push and it squeaked open on its hinges.

Ariele was suddenly torn between following Zelda and going on a hunt for Blanche. But one glimpse of the room Zelda had entered brought her to a quick decision, and she followed the woman inside.

The room was lined with glass-fronted cabinets that were filled to the brim with glassware and assorted dishes and knick-knacks. As she took in the sight, Ariele noted that one particular cabinet held a collection of inkwells, undoubtedly the same inkwells that were now the property of the Larkspur Historical Society.

Zelda set her handbag by the door and clumped across the room. She flung open the door of the largest cabinet, revealing shelves of dishes. All of the dishes were in the same striking blue-and-white pattern.

Reaching up, Zelda took down a platter from the top shelf. "What do you think, Miss Harwood?" Her hands trembled as she held the platter aloft, and her eyes glowed with a strange excitement. "Isn't it absolutely magnificent?"

Ariele inspected the platter. "It's very beautiful," she concurred, which it was, though she'd never had much interest in fancy dishes.

"Yes. It's Spode," Zelda said in an almost reverent whisper. She clutched the dish to her chest. "Let me explain why I wanted you to see this," she said, her voice normal again. "You're obviously uncomfortable accepting the piano as a free gift. So why don't we make a trade?"

Ariele regarded Zelda warily. "What kind of trade?"

"The Spode, of course, in exchange for the piano."

Ariele was momentarily taken aback. Swap a plate for the piano? It seemed too simple a request. "I suppose I could agree to that. You take the platter and I'll keep the piano."

Zelda gave a coarse laugh. Her whole body shook so that her hat nearly fell off her head. "Miss Harwood," she said when she'd regained her composure, "I didn't say the *platter*. I said the *Spode*." She flung her arm out in a gesture that took in the entire cabinet.

A knot formed and tightened in Ariele's stomach as she realized she'd just been royally duped. The collection of dishes must be worth a mint. It was a moment before she became aware that Zelda was still talking: ". . . the boxes that I conveniently carry with me when I travel. I'll bring them in and get the housemaid to help me pack the Spode."

Ariele had had enough. This time she was going to stand her ground. "You'll do no such thing. You may not remove any dish from this room except for the platter."

"And you believe you're going to stop me?" Zelda's eyes blazed with defiance.

Yes! Ariele wanted to scream — even if it meant physically putting herself between Zelda and the cabinet filled with Spode. But she immediately recognized how crazy the idea was. She might be far younger than Zelda, but there was no question that, despite her thinness, Zelda had the strength of a horse. Besides, she reasoned, she had never out of anger laid her hands on anyone in her life. Was she going to start now with a contentious old woman who would be sure to sue for bodily harm if the new mistress of Sheldrake so much as breathed on her?

Ariele contented herself with glaring back at Zelda. Then she turned away, walked out of the room, and headed off to warn Emma. But she stopped short of the kitchen door. What good would it do to order Emma not to help in packing the dishes? Wasn't Zelda apt to override the order with dictates of her own? Though she couldn't fathom that Emma would be fond of the Pilchard sisters, she wasn't entirely sure of the housekeeper's loyalties.

Standing in the hallway, Ariele came to a decision. Fine, she thought, let Zelda take the Spode, let her think she had gotten away with her little trick. Ditto for Blanche, should she also try to cart off something that was not hers. Van was executor of the estate. Let him be the one to handle the affair.

Ariele had no doubt that Van was perfectly capable of putting the sisters in their places. He had already demonstrated his disdain for them. Indeed, Zelda may have met her match in the peppery attorney. The thought made Ariele smile; she wished she could be present when he confronted the sisters. Maybe she would be.

But just because she wouldn't stop Zelda or Blanche didn't mean she couldn't keep an eye on them. With clear purpose now, Ariele started off to look for the stout sister, and she believed she knew where she would find her.

Mounting the steps, Ariele went straight to Elizabeth Sheldrake's private suite. She hesitated outside the closed door for an instant, then opened it wide, expecting to catch a flustered Blanche rummaging through a closet or dresser drawer.

But there was no sign of Blanche in the room, nor any indication that anything had been disturbed. Slightly disappointed, Aricle checked out the small parlor. Nothing appeared to be missing there, either.

During her brief inspection, Ariele purposely avoided glancing at the picture of her aunt that hung on the wall, though she could see its frame from the corner of her eye and knew the portrait hadn't been touched. She bent to try the latch on the trunk; it was secure. After that, she left the suite and made a tour of the other bedrooms. When she saw that they were vacant too, she returned downstairs to the main parlor.

In the parlor, Ariele's efforts were finally met with success. Blanche was seated placidly on the sofa in the same spot she'd occupied before. She gazed up at Ariele with an expression of innocent surprise.

Ariele forced herself to be civil. "Did you find what you were after?"

"Yes," Blanche replied shortly, "but it wasn't a bit satisfactory." Her expression changed into one of distaste.

"What wasn't?"

Blanche threw up her hands. "Why, the dining table and chairs. How can I possibly take them? They're all broken down."

"I'm sure you could find someone to fix them."

Blanche clucked under her breath. "A waste of money. Besides, the set won't fit in our wagon."

Ariele tried to imagine what kind of "wagon" the sisters owned. A Mack truck, maybe? "Perhaps Mr. Caulfield could arrange for delivery."

"No, no, it won't do." Blanche rose from the sofa, holding her handbag against her.

"I'll show you what I must have in place of the set. My dear sister Elizabeth promised it to me days . . . mere days before she . . . died." Blanche choked on the words.

Ariele silently granted the Pilchard sisters one thing. They were superb actresses.

Once she'd dabbed at her eyes with a handkerchief she had produced from her handbag, Blanche assumed an air of command and led Ariele down the hallway to the staircase.

They were near the top of the steps when Ariele heard the sound of the front door slamming. She peered down and saw Zelda, her arms burdened with a stack of boxes.

"Blanche? Blanche! Where are you?"

At Zelda's sharp inquiry, Blanche froze on the steps. She turned around and, with a tentative wave at her sister, said, "Here, Zelda. I'm taking Miss Harwood to the Green Room."

The Green Room? Ariele surmised it must be the one with the hideously peeling paint and water spots the size of giant turtles on the ceiling.

"Never mind, Blanche," her sister said with impatience. "I wanted you to help me, but I'll get the maid instead."

Blanche gave a little shrug, then continued on into the upstairs hallway, with Ariele tagging behind. She stopped at a closed door — the door to the room with the peeling paint, just as Ariele had suspected. "This is it," Blanche announced. She flung open the door and signaled for her companion to go ahead of her.

Like a fat little pigeon, Blanche homed in on one of the room's shroud-covered furnishings. She plucked off the cloth, revealing a small oak vanity. "Isn't it divine?" she enthused.

Ariele thought the vanity hardly warranted such a glowing term as "divine." But, like the Spode, it was probably worth oodles of money. "So you would like to have the dressing table rather than the dining set?"

"Yes, oh yes! And I *must* take it with me today, Miss Harwood."

Ariele was tempted for a second to protest. She doubted that Blanche would have the spunk to challenge her. Blanche was sure, though, to call for her sister, and the small table hardly seemed to Ariele worth the trouble of facing off with Zelda again. So she said, "All right, but you'll have to carry it downstairs yourself."

Blanche drew herself up. "Of course," she huffed. Turning away, she gave her broad backside to Ariele as she bent to examine some detail on the vanity.

Ariele left Blanche to her devices and went to check on Zelda's progress. But Zelda was nowhere to be seen. She wasn't in the room where the Spode was stashed, though Emma was there. The housekeeper stood in a sea of boxes, looking bewildered.

Emma brightened considerably when she saw Ariele. "Miss Harwood, thank goodness you're here." She stepped gingerly around a box. "Is it true that I'm to pack up the Spode for Miss Pilchard?"

Ariele was gratified for Emma's sudden show of trust. She hoped what she had to say didn't diminish it. "Yes, it's true, Emma. For the present," she emphasized.

Her hint must have gotten through. Emma's plain face broke out in a smile. "I see. Well, I'll get right to work."

Ariele watched as Emma began to take down the dishes from the nearest shelf of the cabinet. Then she hit upon an idea. Why not station herself by the front door? That way, she would be in a better position to monitor the sisters' comings and goings. It seemed a good bet, and so she went to set up her post.

The plan worked for a time. Ariele even

found amusement in observing Blanche's awkward progress down the steps, her new vanity in tow. The stout sister put on a convincing act, lumbering and wheezing her way along. In passing, she cast Ariele a pitiful glance — which Ariele gleefully ignored.

But Ariele's amusement fled when Blanche did an about-face and entered the hallway instead of dragging the vanity out the front door. She started to follow Blanche at a discreet distance. Finally, Blanche arrived at the other end of the corridor where a door was standing open. Ariele caught a glimpse of green grass and blue sky. That meant the door led outside.

Just as Blanche began to shove the vanity through the doorway, Ariele heard the heavy thud of footsteps coming up from behind her. She whirled around; to her horror, she saw Zelda bearing down on her at break-neck speed, a huge box clasped in her arms.

Ariele searched desperately for a place to get out of Zelda's way, but there was no escape with Blanche effectively blocking the doorway. A collision seemed inevitable. Panicked, Ariele cried out, "Stop!" Zelda screeched to a halt with a loud whoop and a cry. The box came to rest inches from Ariele's nose.

Ariele began to tremble. Zelda's face, peering around the side of the box, was ashen. "You frightened me nearly to death, Miss Harwood," she accused. Then her countenance suddenly changed, and she appeared to be her old self again. She sniffed. "This is almost the last of it, Miss Harwood. If you'll excuse me . . ."

With that, Zelda maneuvered around Ariele, and the box missed hitting Ariele by a hair, no more. Undeterred, Ariele went after Zelda. At the door she came up short, blinking in stunned surprise at what she saw outside. Parked a few feet from the house was a hearse. An old, ugly-looking black hearse with sagging yellowed curtains at the windows and its back door standing ajar. So that was the sisters' "wagon."

Blanche was at the vehicle, pushing the vanity into its interior. She gave her sister an odd smile and the two exchanged words, which Ariele couldn't make out. Then Blanche took the box from Zelda and deposited it in the back of the vehicle.

Ariele shuddered and turned away. She'd seen enough. She traversed the corridor to the parlor. After the air of confusion created by the Pilchard sisters, the manor seemed unnaturally dark and cool and si-

117

lent. Even the parlor was less inviting than usual to Ariele. She collapsed onto the love seat. Her head felt like there was a tight band around it. Was she going to get a headache? She hoped that Emma kept aspirin in the house.

Sagging back against the plush cushions, Ariele attempted to relax. She made herself think pleasant thoughts of Providence and her apartment and Greenswell Community College, where she worked.

The tightness at her temples gradually eased, but images of Zelda and Blanche kept intruding on the more peaceful ones. She could easily think of several choice words to describe the sisters' actions today. But what concerned her more was how far they were willing to go to seize possession of Sheldrake. Van had assured her there was nothing to worry about in that regard. At the moment Ariele wasn't so sure.

A knock sounded at the parlor door. Ariele automatically tensed in response. Had the sisters returned to raise more havoc? When she got up the courage to look, she saw that it was Emma standing in the doorway. "I came to ask if you'd like some lunch," the housekeeper said, producing a tray.

Ariele at once wondered what time it

was. Her eyes went first to the mantel clock. It wasn't there. That meant the sisters had taken it — and without a fuss.

"Are you hungry?" Emma set the tray in front of Ariele. "It's past noon, you know."

Ariele checked her watch. It was one-fifteen on the nose. "Yes, I am, now that you mention it." She saw that the tray contained a ham sandwich, a green salad, and a glass of lemonade. "Have the sisters gone?" she asked, taking a bite of the sandwich.

Emma nodded. "Left a little while ago. I expect Mr. Caulfield will be here soon, though."

"Yes, I expect he will," Ariele agreed.

But neither of them knew how soon. Emma had no more than gone out of the parlor when Van came in.

Ariele slowly lowered the sandwich to the tray on her lap and watched, slightly mesmerized, as Van strode across the room to her.

He placed his hands on his hips. His eyes flashed danger signals when they met hers. "All right," he demanded, "where are they?"

Chapter Seven

For the first time that day, Ariele felt like smiling. Not only was Van enormously appealing to her in the particular stance he had struck, she realized that his frustration and anger weren't directed at her, but toward the Pilchard sisters. "If you mean Zelda and Blanche," she replied, "they just left. I'm glad you're here, though," she couldn't resist adding.

A little look of pleasure danced across Van's features. Then it disappeared. "So why don't I sit down and you can tell me what happened."

Ariele watched covertly as Van made himself at home on the sofa. Today he wore a jet black sports jacket — in leather, of course — and matching pants. The suit was well set off by a pale yellow shirt and diamond-patterned tie. Despite the predominance of leather, it was proper enough attire for a counselor, Ariele decided, while not so conservative that it hid that counselor's spectacular build.

"I was in court this morning," the counselor in question offered as he rolled up his shirtsleeves to the elbow.

"Then you didn't try to call me around nine or so?" Ariele took a sip of her lemonade.

"No. Should I have?"

Ariele smiled again. Van's hair was slightly mussed. She concluded that it lent him an air of innocence. That was, until Zelda's cutting remark about his use of the opposite sex played through her mind. She cleared her throat. "Zelda claimed that she'd asked you to phone me about a change in plans, that she and Blanche would be coming to the estate this morning instead of in the afternoon."

Van scowled, and the air of innocence departed. "Zelda dished you a lie. But I imagine you've guessed that by now." Leaning forward, he locked his hands together over his knees. "When I got back from court, I learned that the sisters had shown up earlier. Darcy said they hotfooted it out the door as soon as they found out I wouldn't be available until after lunch." He ran a hand through his hair, taming the unruly strands. "I did try to call you half an hour ago. Your line was busy."

"Not busy, Van. The line's dead, though

I assume it was in working order before."

"Dead?" He looked puzzled. "Did you try the extension in the library?"

"I didn't know there was a phone in the library."

"There is, but we'll check that out later. Why don't you continue with your story — and eat your lunch at the same time." He grinned. "I wouldn't want you to go hungry."

The way he was staring at her, Ariele suddenly felt a different kind of hunger, one that she promptly forced herself to dismiss. Between bites of sandwich and salad, she related the morning's events to him.

Van appeared to be listening raptly. But as soon as Ariele told him about Zelda and the Spode, his expression darkened. "How did she get into that room?" he broke in sharply.

The question struck Ariele as redundant. "How do you think? She opened the door and walked in."

"Wrong!" Van jumped up from the sofa, startling Ariele. "That room — the rear parlor, Elizabeth called it — stays locked." He punctuated his point by jabbing the air with his index finger.

Ariele wondered if that was his usual demeanor in court. If so, she'd love to see him conduct a case. "But Zelda got in somehow," she argued. "Remember, I was there."

"Yes." Van paced the length of the room and back. "As far as I know, there are only two keys to the rear parlor. I have one of them. The other's now in your possession, on the ring you took from the deposit box."

"Oh." A disturbing possibility entered Ariele's mind, and it was her turn to spring up from her seat. "Excuse me for a minute." She hurried out before he could protest.

She rushed upstairs to the guest room and went straight to her purse. Unzipping it, she turned the purse upside down and shook out its contents. Frantically, she searched through the jumble of lipstick cases, scraps of paper, and spare change that seemed to have become permanent inhabitants of the bottom of her purse. She was rewarded at last when her fingers closed around the ring of keys.

Ariele let out a sigh of relief. Her fear that Zelda had stolen the keys was unfounded. Then it occurred to her that there'd hardly been an opportunity for Zelda to take the keys — at least not before she gained entry into the rear parlor.

Sheepishly Ariele trotted downstairs and explained her actions to Van. His response was to smile and say, "Was that the problem? I thought maybe your lunch didn't agree with you."

Ariele laughed. But her humor quickly faded. "How do you suppose Zelda got hold of a key?"

Van came and settled himself on the arm of the love seat. "That's a very good question, and one I hope to have an answer to real soon." He regarded Ariele. "I don't want to hurry you, but are you about finished eating?"

She looked at the remains of her meal. "I'm done." She glanced at Van. "I'm sorry. I didn't ask if you'd had your lunch. I'm sure Emma would be glad to make you a sandwich."

"Sounds tempting, but I grabbed a burger in town. However . . ." He got up, and Ariele rose too so that they were facing each other. "Emma invited me to stay for dinner this evening. I said I'd need your okay first. Do I have it?"

Standing so near to him, how could she refuse his request? "It would be great if you stayed for dinner." As soon as the words were out, questions filled her mind. What would Darcy's reaction be if she

124

knew of the plans? Maybe Van had told her he was having dinner with a client. Wasn't that what she was?

Van interrupted her thoughts. "I was hoping you'd say that," he replied softly. "Now let's see about the phone in the library, and you can finish your tale of Zelda and the Spode, though I'm not sure I want to hear how it ends."

"I'll relate every sinister detail," Ariele teased, and proceeded to do just that. When she mentioned the sisters' wagon, Van laughed.

"I probably should have warned you."

"But it suits them, don't you think?"

"I'm afraid it does."

Van showed her the location of the phone in the library. She wasn't surprised she'd overlooked it before, since it was nearly hidden between two of the bookcases.

Van held the receiver to his ear. "The line's dead, all right," he announced. He took something from his pants pocket. It appeared to be a wallet, but when he unfolded it, Ariele saw that the object was a slim cellular phone.

"I'm calling Darcy," he explained. "She can report the outage to the phone company. Hopefully, you'll have your service restored by tomorrow."

Though she knew it was only a business call, Ariele moved away from him while he talked to Darcy. She let her gaze roam over the room, her mind idly registering the various details — the bookcases lined from end to end with books, the little table with its vase and alabaster bust, a tall fern in a pot that she hadn't noticed before. *Something wasn't right about the room.* At first she couldn't say what it was. Her eyes studied the various furnishings again, and she saw the problem. It was the table. No, not the table itself, she realized, but what was missing from it. "Van," she called.

He came up beside her. "What's wrong?"

Ariele gave a nervous swallow. "Yesterday, there was an alabaster bust of a young girl on this table." She touched the tabletop. "Now it's gone."

Van folded the phone and shoved it into his pocket. "Are you sure that's where it was?"

"Positive. I moved it so that I could stack some books there. The sculpture caught my attention because it was so attractive. Before I left the library, I put it back in the exact same place I'd found it."

"There could be a logical explanation, you know. Maybe Emma was cleaning in here and moved the sculpture."

But Ariele didn't hear what he said. Her mind had raced ahead to another possibility. "Blanche!" She unconsciously tugged at Van's sleeve. "Blanche must have taken the sculpture." She had no trouble at all picturing the stout sister stuffing the statue into her handbag.

"How do you figure that?" Van asked.

"Because when Zelda carted me off to see the Spode, Blanche disappeared. Zelda claimed that there was nothing to worry about, that — these were her exact words — 'Blanche adores going off on her own.' Besides . . ." She just then noticed she had a death grip on Van's sleeve. Murmuring an embarrassed apology, she let go of him.

Van grinned. "Besides," he prompted.

"The sisters had handbags this big." She sketched the dimensions in the air for him.

His eyebrows arched; he whistled under his breath. "That big, huh?"

Ariele giggled, but Van turned contemplative. Without warning, his hand caught hers. "Don't worry. I'll take care of the sisters. Remember, their prize jewels are locked away in the deposit box."

Ariele wondered if he was planning on holding the pins hostage until Zelda returned the Spode. But her attention was more centered on the warm feeling of his fingers wrapped around hers and the idea that her small hand fit perfectly in his larger one. Before she could consider the implications of that, Van dropped her hand.

"Come with me," he said. "I want to check something outside." He made fast strides for the hallway, and Ariele had to move quickly to catch up to him.

Van circled the manor, finally stopping beside a large snowball bush that was under a window. He hunkered down, his back to Ariele. For a moment all she could see was his red hair, his broad shoulders. It was a very pleasant view, though she did wonder what he was doing.

He motioned for her to join him. "Here's your problem." He held up a piece of black tubing that was hanging loose from the house.

"What is it?"

"The telephone line. It's been cut . . . or gnawed in two by a critter with very sharp teeth."

Whether or not he'd meant the last as a joke was lost on Ariele. Her eyes were fixed on the wire. "Cut? You mean that someone did it on purpose?"

There was no humor in Van's voice when he said, "That's my guess. The wire's cleanly severed."

Ariele could think of just one explanation. "Do you believe that Zelda and Blanche . . ."

"Do I believe that Zelda and Blanche are capable of such a stunt?" Van looked at her. Then his attention seemed diverted elsewhere. "Here's something." He indicated a patch of bare ground directly below the dangling wire.

The spot was shaded by the bush, and Ariele had to squint to see the imprint that was visible on the damp earth. The print was not well defined, but she guessed that it had been made by the toe of a shoe or a boot.

"By chance did you happen to notice what kind of shoes Zelda and Blanche were wearing?" Van asked quietly.

Ariele shook her head with dismay. "That was the one thing about them that I didn't pay any attention to."

"Too bad." He got up, and Ariele followed.

"What are we going to do?" she said, more troubled than she wanted to admit at the idea that the Pilchard sisters would stoop to acts of vandalism.

Van brushed at his pants, though they didn't appear to have any dirt on them. "We could — probably should — call the sheriff's office. If we do, they'll send an officer out. He'll ask us some questions, inspect the phone wire, take photos of the print — for what it's worth. He might pay a visit to Zelda and Blanche, quiz them a little."

He didn't sound very enthusiastic, and Ariele herself wasn't keen on notifying the authorities. But she had to ask, "Do you think it would do any good?"

"Put yourself in the officer's shoes. You know that Zelda and Blanche Pilchard have been generous patrons of the Burroughs County Sheriff's Benevolent Society for more years than you've been alive. Neither of them has ever been accused of any type of criminal mischief in their seventy- or eighty-odd years. Are you going to call into question their integrity, tell them they're suspected of theft, not to mention destruction of property?"

He'd clearly made his point. Ariele, however, had another concern. "What if they have other keys? Suppose they can gain access to the front or back doors?"

"I think you'd be prudent to have the locks changed."

"Good idea. But since I'll soon be putting Sheldrake in the hand of a real estate agent, won't he take care of that by putting lockboxes on the doors?"

Van's eyes held hers for what seemed a very long time. "That's true. But only if you're still determined to sell the estate."

Why did he keep doubting her intentions? It raised her ire again, and she looked away from him. "Isn't it about time I showed you the carousel?" she asked stiffly.

"I thought you'd never ask," he shot back.

They walked together in silence, each keeping a small, but definite distance from the other. Yet Ariele had never been more aware of Van's presence, of the vitality that he projected — or her response to it. If only he were that older attorney that she'd envisioned when she'd seen his name on the letter informing her of her inheritance, an inheritance that was threatening to give her major headaches. Why had her nice, sane life been thrown such an unexpected curve?

"Which way do we go?"

Van's voice intruded on her thoughts, and Ariele saw that they'd come to the place where the stone path divided into the two trails. "This way." She indicated the appropriate trail and went ahead of Van. Somehow the ice had been broken again, and she told him about seeing the gardener's cottage. That seemed to lead naturally into relating the details of her unexpected encounter with Denton in the parlor.

Van's steps slowed to a stop, and he turned to her. "What was he doing in there?"

"I'm not sure. He'd come from the kitchen. He had a package in his hands from Emma. Apparently, she'd given him some food to take home." Ariele hesitated, recalling the sense of uneasiness that had come over her in Denton's presence. "He didn't say much to me, just went out through the glass doors and, I assume, on to his cottage."

"He had no business coming through the parlor," Van responded tersely. "If he was in the kitchen, he should have left through the back door. I'll speak to him about it."

Ariele wondered if that was necessary, but she said nothing. "I locked the parlor doors after he was gone. I don't know why they'd been unlocked."

Van appeared thoughtful. "I don't know either."

They resumed walking again. "Do you know much about Denton, how my aunt happened to hire him?"

"She hired him shortly before she got

sick. Her former gardener, Charles, had given notice. He'd been at Sheldrake quite a few years and was ready to retire and move south to live near his daughter."

"Then Denton hasn't been at Sheldrake very long. What's your impression of him?"

"Quiet, kind of a loner. He seems to know his work pretty well. He does a decent job on the grounds."

"I think so too," she agreed, but she couldn't shake the strange feelings of uncertainty the subject of the gardener provoked in her. "Do you know what was wrong with my aunt?" she asked, switching to a subject that was only slightly less disturbing.

Van stared straight ahead. "Cancer, I believe," he said at last. "Elizabeth never told me. She was an attractive woman for her age, Ariele. Intelligent, alert. But she was a private woman too."

Ariele could understand that. She thought of the cruel remark Zelda had made. "Zelda told me that my aunt was in a confused state of mind." She looked sideways at Van. "Was she like that . . . toward the end?"

"Yes, she was," Van acknowledged. "Undoubtedly, it was caused by the drugs the doctor gave her for the pain." He studied

Ariele's face. "I don't think she suffered badly for more than a few weeks. And I can assure you she was in a perfectly sound state of mind when she made out her will."

Ariele shook her head. "No, I wasn't thinking of the will. It's just . . ." She searched for the right words. "It just struck me that Zelda seemed to enjoy the idea that her half-sister had suffered. And though I hadn't thought much about my aunt before, now that I'm here, I find myself wishing more and more that I could have known her. Does that make sense?"

"It makes perfect sense," Van responded. "And you can still come to know her, if you give yourself the chance."

Ariele wanted to ask him what he meant, but they'd arrived at the bench and rose arbor, and so she shared with him her idea that the area had been a formal garden.

"It was," Van replied, "and could be again."

She let the last remark go by. The thicket stood in front of them, and with the sun shining so brightly overhead, she was able to spot the carousel horse that she'd mistaken for a statue. She pointed it out to Van.

"Yes, I see," he said.

Together, they peered into the thicket.

Then Van pressed forward, clearing away a tangle of dead branches that blocked their way. "Through here." He motioned to Ariele.

Following him into the thicket, Ariele was astonished to discover that it wasn't a mass of briars and bramble bushes, as she'd imagined it would be. Instead there was plenty of space for both Van and herself to move around, and sufficient light filtered through to illuminate the small merry-go-round. "This is like a little room," she said finally, her voice hushed.

Van smiled. "It even has a roof." He indicated the dilapidated roof with its canopy of leaves and vines.

Ariele reached out and touched the horse that was closest to her. Most of its paint had worn off, but enough clung to the animal so that she could tell it had once been white with a pink-and-blue bridle and saddle. Anxious for Van's opinion, she asked, "What do you think of it?"

He flaked off a piece of the pink paint and held it in his hand. "I think . . ." He shook his head. "I think the carousel's fantastic, Ariele." Taking her hand in his, he placed the paint chip in her palm.

Ariele studied the chip. "I wonder where

the merry-go-round came from and how old it is . . . and why it's here."

"I wish I knew."

She crumbled the paint chip between her fingers and let the dust fall onto the buckled wooden floor. "My aunt never mentioned it to you?"

"Not so much as a hint." Van walked partway around the carousel, stopping to inspect one of the horses that was on its side.

Ariele joined him, watching as he tore away a twisted portion of vine that encircled the animal's neck and threw it aside. "All of this could be restored," he said.

His face was turned from her so that she couldn't read his eyes. "Maybe whoever buys Sheldrake will want to fix it up." She thought of the Larkspur Historical Society. Even if her aunt hadn't been overly fond of its president or his idea to turn the manor into a museum, if he and his society made a good offer on the estate, she could hardly refuse it.

"The carousel could be a selling point too, you know." Van made eye contact with her. "I could do most of the work myself. It would be fun, a challenge."

She was taken aback by his offer. "It would?"

Van smiled. "Don't look so shocked, Ariele. I've got quite a bit of experience in construction. I believe I could tackle something like this with a fair amount of success."

She was curious as to how he'd come to know so much about building things. She was going to ask him, when he said, "Why are you in such a hurry to leave here?"

The question took her off guard, and she didn't respond at once. Van came nearer to her until their bodies were almost touching. "Is it because of your job?" He paused for a heartbeat. "Or is it because someone's waiting for you in Providence?"

Ariele tried to evade both the man and his prying questions, but she only succeeded in putting herself in a worse position. In effect, she was wedged between Van and the toppled horse. Van's breath was now a hot caress on her cheek; the heady scent of his cologne filled her nostrils. How was a woman supposed to think clearly under such circumstances?

"Well?" Van's gaze, sky blue, penetrated hers.

She couldn't bring herself to lie to him, to say that she was due back at her post at the college when in truth she had the summer off because the school was on minimal staff until September. And she couldn't tell him that it was because she had "someone" waiting for her return.

"No . . . on both counts," she said at last. "I'm not working this summer. And at the moment I'm not seriously involved with anyone in Providence, if that's what you meant." She was more than slightly tempted to question his status in that regard.

Van's expression put off any inquiry she might have gathered the courage to make about his love life. "That's precisely what I meant," he said. "So why don't you consider staying for a month or two?"

Fleetingly Ariele thought about the activities she had planned for the summer — the reading she'd hoped to catch up on; a nonpaying job as a tour guide at the Fine Arts Center; tennis and swimming with a couple of close friends who also had the summer off; a trip to Wisconsin to visit a cousin who had moved there a year ago. Suddenly none of them seemed that urgent or exciting, and she found herself wavering. "Is there any reason for me to stay longer at Sheldrake?" she hedged.

"Perhaps. Do you remember I told you there were possibilities for the estate, besides selling it?"

"Like what?" A little surge of excitement went through her. She tried in vain to squelch it.

"For starters, how about a bed-and-breakfast inn?"

"A . . ." That idea, at least, was absurd.

Van folded his arms across his chest. "Yes, an inn. It was a dream your aunt had."

"But I don't have a clue as to how to run an inn. I'm a librarian, in case you've forgotten."

Van flashed his trademark grin. "I haven't forgotten. But I know a thing or two about operating a B-and-B. My sister and her husband own one in Pennsylvania. I helped them out for a few summers while I was attending Harvard."

Harvard. Ariele digressed from the subject at hand. Van didn't look Ivy League, though he was obviously a man of intelligence and savvy. Had he worn leather on campus? The thought made her smile.

"What's so funny?"

She waved him off. "Nothing. Just a thought I had."

"I'm very interested in your thoughts, Ariele." His hand came up to rest against the horse's head, a hair's breadth from her arm. "What am I going to have to do to convince you?" he asked huskily, his eyes focused on her lips. "Kiss you?"

"I . . . hardly think this conversation is appropriate," she stammered, seeking once more to distance herself from him.

Ariele didn't succeed, and she was forced to realize that it was because she didn't want to escape him, after all. A picture of the rose arbor and bench came, unbidden, into her mind. A picture too of a young Elizabeth Sheldrake, sitting on the bench in the midst of her formal garden. And she wasn't alone. A man was with her — the man whose face Ariele had glimpsed in the locket, the man whose kiss she imagined that Elizabeth longed for.

All at once Ariele knew it was really she who longed to be kissed — not by the mysterious man in the locket, but here and now by Van. She pushed aside every doubt, every comparison she might feel compelled to make between Van and Jerod. She ignored every warning that tumbled through her mind and told her she was a fool for giving in to her impulses. She waited until Van's arms came around her, pulling her against himself. He whispered her name. Then she freely lifted her face to his and let his mouth claim hers.

The kiss was dazzlingly intense, but

brief. When it ended, she clung to Van, eyes closed. "Your answer," he said, his lips brushing her ear.

For a moment Ariele found it impossible to form a coherent sentence, though she was positive of one thing. Van Caulfield was a very persuasive man. *Like Jerod.* No, she decided. Jerod hadn't gone to Harvard; he had flunked out of community college, in fact. As far as she'd known, Jerod hadn't had an ambition in the world, except to have a good time. The last she had heard, his father was still supporting him.

Van moved her a bit away from himself, though his arms still held her tight. "Don't you know you've put yourself in peril by keeping me in suspense?"

Ariele raised an eyebrow. "Is that what you call it? I would say that your present conduct is hardly professional, Mr. Caulfield."

"That may be true, Miss Harwood, but in case you hadn't noticed, my interest in you surpasses professional boundaries."

She had noticed; that was a large part of her dilemma. Another part had to do with her own confused emotions and her stubborn suspicion that Van was involved with his receptionist. If it were true, what business did he have kissing one of his clients?

And what business did that client have responding in such an enthusiastic manner?

"Well, Ariele?"

Van's persistence brought her around to his original question, and she found herself weakening. "I suppose that I could arrange to spend a couple of extra weeks at Sheldrake," she conceded.

"You're aware, aren't you, that it'll take you twice that long to inventory your new library?"

"I'm not aware of that at all," she retorted. But she had to admit he'd made an excellent point.

Van's arms finally released her. But not his eyes. "I was serious about restoring the carousel," he said, his gaze locked with hers. "That goes whether or not you keep the estate." He left her to inspect one of the other horses. "I have most of the tools at home that we'd need to get started," he said over his shoulder.

"You mean I would help you . . . assuming that I agreed to your suggestion?" Which she didn't want him to think she was doing. "I have to warn you that I might be a distraction. I'm helpless with a hammer, couldn't drive a nail straight if my life depended on it."

Van returned to her and took her chin in

his hand. His thumb lightly skimmed her lower lip. "Ariele, you're the kind of distraction I'd welcome," he said amiably. "And don't worry. You won't be using either a hammer or nails. Maybe a paintbrush." He let go of her. "But why do I get the impression that you fear Sheldrake — the manor, to be specific — is about to fall down?"

"Isn't it?"

"Actually, the house is in good condition. You've already discovered that the plumbing works. Most of the pipes were replaced a few years ago, and Elizabeth had a larger water heater installed. The furnace is nearly new too, something you'll learn to appreciate if you're here in the winter." He shoved his hands in his pants pockets. "Although there are other, more enjoyable ways to keep warm," he said with a smile.

With the taste of him still on her lips, Ariele didn't dare ask him what those other ways were. "What about the roof?" she said, struggling to keep her mind on the practical.

"The roof's in pretty bad shape," he agreed.

"And the upstairs bedrooms, excluding the guest room?"

He brightened. "The problems in those rooms are mostly cosmetic. Some paint, wallpaper, fresh plaster in a couple of places should make a considerable difference."

"The expense?"

"Not bad." Her skepticism must have shown, for he laughed. "I'm afraid I'll have to explain that over dinner." He consulted his watch. "As much as I don't want to leave you, I've got to get back to the office."

Though she didn't want him to go, she said, "All right."

Before they left the thicket, they took one last look around. Ariele let herself entertain the notion that it might be fun helping Van fix up the merry-go-round. But she made a valiant attempt to dismiss it as they walked back to the manor.

When they came to the place where the trails merged into one, Van went ahead. Ariele lingered behind a bit, then caught up to him at the edge of the backyard.

Near the house Van stopped abruptly. "Look at that." He sounded disgusted.

Ariele looked where he was pointing — and saw the wide set of tire tracks that had flattened a portion of the grass. She knew they were made by the Pilchard sisters' hearse. The memory of the pair loading the vanity and boxes into the back of the ugly vehicle was all too vivid in her mind.

Just then a cloud slipped in front of the sun, and Ariele's eyes were drawn upward to the manor. Cloaked in shadow, the curtains at its windows shut fast, the old home appeared fortresslike and somber. She could easily picture the sisters inside, plundering its secrets and taking whatever booty pleased them, and she shuddered inwardly.

Van must have sensed her thoughts, for he touched her arm and urged her on, and together they went into the manor.

Chapter Eight

After Van left, Ariele went upstairs. Since she had an hour or so before dinner, she would have time to change her clothes and refresh her makeup.

She found a clean set of towels and washcloths laid out on the bed. Collecting them, she grabbed her makeup kit from the drawer and set off for the bathroom. While she applied her lipstick and blush, she tried not to think about what had happened at the carousel, about Van's kiss — and her enthusiastic response to it. Still, she couldn't deny that his kiss, his very presence in her life at this moment had caused her to cast common sense aside and commit herself to staying on at Sheldrake longer than was necessary. While it might be true that her discovery of the merry-go-round had been intriguing, if she were honest she'd have to admit that Van's offer to restore it intrigued her in a different way.

And what about his suggestion that Sheldrake would make an ideal bed-and-breakfast inn? Even though she regarded the notion as totally absurd, hadn't she already begun to see the manor in a more favorable light? With a sigh, she hurried to finish her task. Then she went back to her room and slipped on her pink dress.

She was just giving her reflection a final check when she heard the roar of The Litigator in the lane. Looking out, she saw the motorcycle glide to a stop beside her car. But whose car was that parked on the other side of her Honda? Was it Emma's? More likely, the car belonged to the gardener, she thought.

Ariele watched a moment longer as Van dismounted The Litigator and went through his little ritual of hanging his helmet upside down and depositing his gloves in it. When he started across the lawn, she went downstairs to meet him.

Van's gaze caught hers as soon as she opened the door. "Hello," he said, and the word seemed to her more than a simple greeting.

"Hi," she said. "Would you like to wait in the parlor or . . ."

At that moment Emma appeared in the foyer. Her cheeks were flushed pink. "Dinner's ready," she announced.

A murmur of appreciation rose from

Ariele's lips when she stepped into the dining room. Emma had wrought a minor miracle, transforming the austere room into one that was almost cozy. She'd accomplished this by covering the table with a white lace cloth and placing a bouquet of flowers and a lighted candelabra in the center. At one end of the table two place settings were situated intimately opposite each other.

"The table looks beautiful, Emma."

The housekeeper's face radiated pleasure. "Glad you think so, Miss Harwood." She turned to pick up a pitcher that was on the sideboard. "Perhaps you and Mr. Caulfield would like some iced tea while you're waiting for me to bring in your meal." She set the pitcher on the table and left the room.

Van pulled out Ariele's chair for her, then seated himself. He filled both their glasses with the tea.

Ariele regarded him over her glass as she sipped her tea. He'd been right when he'd said candles could be romantic under certain circumstances. Just now she was admiring the burnished quality his hair took on in the soft light. She wondered how it would feel to run her fingers through it. "Did you have dinner often with my aunt?" she asked.

148

"Not often. A few times a year."

"You enjoyed her company though, I assume."

"Anyone with an appreciation for intelligent, stimulating conversation would have enjoyed Elizabeth's company. Until her illness, she was a very vital woman."

Ariele set her glass on the table. "How did you come to be her attorney?"

Van hesitated, yet he didn't appear uncomfortable with the question. Just as he seemed about to make a reply, Emma bustled into the room.

"The salad course first." She put a plate of mixed greens on top of Ariele's dinner plate, another one on top of Van's. "I'll be back in a few minutes with the main course," she said.

Ariele and Van briefly occupied themselves with their salads. After he'd eaten several forkfuls, Van wiped his mouth on his napkin and placed his fork across his plate. "As I was about to say, I became Elizabeth's attorney by more or less inheriting the position." He laughed at Ariele's inquisitive glance. "Her former attorney had passed away shortly before I came to Larkspur to set up my practice. His office referred her to me. After an initial consultation, Elizabeth hired me to help her draw

149

up a will. That was four years ago."

It all sounded very reasonable to Ariele. But she picked up on something he'd said. "I gather you're not a native of this area."

"No." He speared a tomato slice with his fork. "I was born and raised in Pittsburgh."

"Why did you choose a small town in upstate New York to practice law?" She would have thought he'd be more at home in a cosmopolitan setting.

"My uncle — Darcy's father, that is — lives here."

The news took a minute to register. When it did, Ariele realized that it meant Van and Darcy were first cousins. Such a close relationship seemed hardly conducive to the two of them being an item. Had she misinterpreted their feelings for each other? "Did your uncle recommend Larkspur to you?"

"He and his family like it here. Let's just say in my case that I was looking for a place to settle down — any place other than Pittsburgh." His voice held a slightly bitter tone.

"You didn't care for Pittsburgh?"

Van lapsed into silence, and Ariele regretted asking the question. They both picked at the remains of their salads.

Finally he said, "My father, Van Caulfield II, owns the largest construction company in Pittsburgh. My grandfather, Van Caulfield I, started the business."

Now Ariele understood where he got his knowledge of building things. "A family affair," she said, sensing that perhaps it wasn't such a satisfactory one.

"Yes, you could say that." Van made an impatient gesture with his hand. "The trouble was that I couldn't have cared less about continuing the tradition."

"Your father expected you to succeed him, of course."

"To put it mildly. And to also put it mildly, I've been a great disappointment to him."

The words caused a gnawing pain in the vicinity of Ariele's heart. "But how could you disappoint him? You're a successful attorney. You —"

"He believes all attorneys are inherently dishonest," Van broke in. "I disagree with him. I suppose you could say that he and I have always walked different beats. His ideas and mine rarely mesh."

"That happens," she said softly.

Van leaned forward; to Ariele's surprise, he reached for her hand. Holding it in his, he studied her palm. "I seemed to have been born with a definite sense of adventure. I've always had the fever to travel, experience whatever came my way."

"Have you traveled?" She was acutely aware of the touch of Van's finger against her skin as he sketched an invisible line down the length of her hand.

Looking up, he said, "To an extent, yes. But this globe's a big, fascinating place. It would take more than a few lifetimes to see and do it all." He slowly withdrew his hand from hers.

Was it what Van had said or the way he had said it? Ariele wasn't sure, but all at once she saw her own life as a bit dull by contrast.

"Something else," he went on with a smile. "From the time I was twelve, I was determined I'd be a lawyer some day. I even saved my allowances to buy a pricey attaché case. Do you know I kept that case and never used it until I received my degree? Now I carry it with me to the office every day. I guess the case serves as a reminder to me that dreams can come true."

"That's wonderful, Van." She meant it, but if he were to ask her what her dreams were, could she tell him? "So you didn't have any interest in running a construction company?" she said, just wanting to hear him talk some more.

"I enjoyed the physical side of it, especially working on site with a crew — which, by the way, is how I spent my summers during high school." He looked reflective. "But I had a more serious reason for walking away from the family business."

"Can you tell me what it was?"

Van fidgeted with his napkin. "My father's a decent guy, and Caulfield Construction has a squeaky-clean reputation around Pittsburgh." He lifted his glass to his lips and finished the tea in it. "Unfortunately, my father's more married to the company than to my mother, more devoted to his employees than he is — or was — to my sister, Rebecca, and me."

His hurt was all too evident to Ariele, and she suspected that beneath those flashy clothes and that brash exterior lay a generous streak of vulnerability. The notion stirred in her an urge to take Van in her arms and soothe him with kisses and comforting words. She knew where the desire came from; kisses and comforting words were something she had longed for many times. Yearning to let him know she understood, she said, "I'm sorry."

Van studied her face for what seemed a very long time. "It's okay. Dad and I made peace of sorts a couple of years ago. And Rebecca's had a better relationship with him since she's gotten married."

"I'm glad to hear that."

"Me too, even if some of our views are still miles apart. Take marriage, for instance." His gaze held hers again. "I made up my mind years ago that when I met the woman I wanted to marry, I was going to be far more devoted to her than to my job." He paused. "There's another thing. I hope the woman who becomes my wife will be someone who, like me, isn't afraid to take a few risks."

Ariele sat up straighter in her chair. She averted her eyes to a distant corner of the room. "I'm sure there are . . . any number of women who meet that . . . criterion." The stupidity of her remark was confirmed when she heard Van chuckle. Only Emma's timely intervention with the main course prevented Ariele from making any further blunders.

She watched as the housekeeper placed a platter of chicken on the table. It was followed by bowls of mashed potatoes, sliced carrots, and squash. Finally Emma set a basket of rolls near Ariele. "There. Can I get you anything else?"

Ariele smiled at the housekeeper. "I don't think so, Emma. It all looks delicious." The food did look appetizing, but Van's words about marriage still rang in Ariele's ears as she occupied herself with buttering two of the rolls. She handed one of the rolls to Van.

"It's great," he said after taking a bite. "Of course, Emma's reputation as a cook is without comparison." His face lit up in a grin. "You know, if you should decide to turn Sheldrake into a bed-and-breakfast, Emma would be ecstatic. She'd have a ball cooking for your guests."

Ariele's hand stopped midway to her mouth. The man obviously loved catching her off-guard. But this time she was ready to dish it back. "You're shameless, Van Caulfield. But you already know that, don't you?"

Van winked in reply, but the brief exchange had served to dispel any lingering tension between them. They heaped their plates with food from the platter and bowls.

"What I told you earlier about the roof," Van said finally, separating a piece of chicken meat from the bone with his fork. "My uncle is a roofer and I guarantee that he'll quote you an excellent price on a new one."

Ariele's response was immediate. "I don't want any favors. After all, I've inherited a fair-size nest egg."

"And I'm not about to let you blow it on shingles and a bucket of tar."

"Since you put it that way, I have to admit it doesn't sound like a very exciting investment."

They both laughed. "Now that we've settled one important matter," he said, "and you've learned about my hang-ups, tell me about yourself. All I know is that you're a librarian and there's no special man in your life at the moment."

He would mention that, she thought. But the speculative look he gave her, the fact that he'd opened up to her, prompted her to talk. "Well, I grew up in Providence and attended Brown University, where I majored in library science."

When Van questioned whether she'd ever thought of living anywhere other than Providence, Ariele confessed she hadn't, that after she was offered the position of assistant to the director of libraries at the college, she'd considered herself fortunate.

"You're happy with your job?"

"Yes, I am." She could say it with confidence. But if she were honest with herself, could she tell him she loved it so much that she could never give it up?

"You told me before that your mother died the year after you'd visited Sheldrake. Your father?"

Ariele folded her napkin in two, then unfolded it. That little ache came back to stab at her heart. "It appears we both had . . . absentee fathers," she said quietly. "Only mine divorced my mother when I was five. He left Providence the same year and I haven't seen him since. About all I know is that he remarried, and he and his wife live in California."

"I'm sorry, Ariele. Do you have other family in Providence?"

"Just a cousin. Shortly after my mother died, I was adopted by my mother's stepbrother and his wife. They were good to me." She stopped, reflecting. "But I never felt really close to them." She didn't add that a few years later Jerod had come into her life, and for a timc shc'd sought escape from her heartache and uncertainty with him.

Van took her hand in his again. "I think I'm beginning to understand why you act fearful of change, why you want your life to be nice and safe."

He didn't know the half of it. But what he'd just said also meant he could see that

157

she wasn't a risk taker — something he considered desirable in a woman. She didn't care; she was proud of the life she'd finally made for herself. Removing her hand from his, she said tightly, "You're only saying that because I've chosen to put Sheldrake up for sale rather than keep it."

Van didn't argue with her, only stared at her in a way that made her feel as if he could see through her pretense and read her very thoughts.

Ariele busied herself with arranging her utensils just so across her empty plate.

"Are you okay?"

She looked up at him. "I'm fine. Why shouldn't I be?" A change in conversation was definitely needed. Besides, there was something she had to ask him. "I do want to know, though, what it is about Archer Winslow that makes you so angry."

It was obvious she'd hit a nerve. Van's eyes darkened. He didn't answer at once. "Be glad you brought the subject up after dinner," he said tersely. "What I have to tell you could have ruined your appetite."

"It's that bad?"

His jaw set in a hard line. "Archer is the owner of Winslow Farms. It's purported to be a horse breeding facility, but I suspect it's more of a front for an illegal betting operation — among other disreputable activities." He regarded her. "Are you aware that Archer's your neighbor?"

"Yes." She was more concerned at the moment with the terms "illegal betting" and "disreputable activities."

Van shoved his dinner plate aside. "About a year ago, there was a fire at Winslow Farms. It destroyed a foaling barn and the two prize colts that occupied the barn."

Ariele gasped in surprise. "No! How tragic." She'd always loved animals and couldn't stand to see them hurt.

"For the colts, yes," Van agreed. "But not for Archer."

"What do you mean?"

"The colts were insured for huge sums of money, Ariele. When they were killed, Archer was extremely well compensated for the loss." His voice held thinly disguised anger.

Ariele didn't blame him. At the same time, a nightmarish possibility came into her mind. "Isn't it usual for a farmer to insure his animals?"

"Of course. It just happened in Archer's case that one of his employees — a foreman in charge of one of the stables — went to the authorities after the fire and told them he had proof the foaling barn had been deliberately torched."

The nightmarish possibility was confirmed. "Arson," she said numbly.

Van looked sullen. "There was an investigation, but nothing conclusive was found. The foreman left the area. Or, I should say, disappeared."

"He didn't leave a forwarding address?"

"No. The sheriff's office tried to trace his whereabouts." Van's mouth twisted in an ironic smile. "Archer was particularly cooperative. He claimed the man had stolen supplies and cash from the farm, then skipped out."

"You don't believe that, do you?"

"No, and neither did the authorities after several employees at the farm vouched for the foreman's honesty. Besides, he had a clean record, no arrests."

A chill went through Ariele. "Are you saying that the foreman might have been murdered?"

Van took the pitcher of tea and refilled his glass. Then he reached for Ariele's, but she shook her head. He set the pitcher aside. "Let's just say that he would have been the star witness if Winslow had been brought to trial for arson. And I would have been one of the prosecuting attorneys on the case."

"I see." There seemed little else for her to say.

"Ariele, the owner of Winslow Farms is a dangerous man. He's after Sheldrake any way he can get his hands on it. Incidentally, you might be interested to know that he and his wife were recently divorced."

She shifted uncomfortably. "He invited himself to sit down with me the other day. His purpose was to tell me that he wanted to buy Sheldrake."

"Don't sell to him."

Though a part of her rebelled at the idea of Van dictating to her what she should or shouldn't do, she understood his reasons. Even if some of what he'd revealed about Archer Winslow was true, there was no way she would let the man take possession of her estate. "I'll be careful," she promised.

"You need to be." Van offered her a tentative smile. "I'm not trying to frighten you."

"No?" Should she be afraid? Another matter weighed on her mind. There seemed no better time to bring it up. "The other day you mentioned that the Larkspur Historical Society would like to turn Sheldrake into a museum. But you also said that my aunt was no fan of Philip

161

Hubbard. Why? Is he a threat to my property too?"

Van settled back in his chair. "I think threat is probably too strong a word. Apparently, Elizabeth's differences with Philip were mostly philosophical. Under his guidance, the Society has become more aggressive in its tactics in recent years. Elizabeth didn't believe in aggression in any form." He smiled. "It's true that Philip has whipped up quite a bit of public support for his museum idea. He's eager, and if he believes he can persuade you to part with Sheldrake for a song, he's game to try."

"I have no intention of selling my estate for a song." Ariele started to say more, but Emma came in.

The housekeeper whisked away their empty plates. "Well, it looks like you're both ready for dessert."

Ariele and Van looked at each other. Then Ariele spoke up. "The meal was wonderful, but I'm afraid I couldn't eat another bite right now."

Emma gave Van an inquisitive glance. "Great cooking, Emma, but I'm full at the moment too."

"Dessert's apple pie," the housekeeper said hopefully.

"Maybe later."

Emma brightened at Ariele's offer. "I'll serve the pie to you in the parlor. You can let me know when you want it."

"Hmm. It seems Emma thinks we'll be in the parlor this evening," Van said when the housekeeper was gone.

The comment drew a smile from Ariele. "So what would you like to do in the parlor — now that we're properly stuffed?"

The way his eyes twinkled in response made her suddenly wish she'd worded the question differently, even if his reply was innocent. "Didn't I promise to show you how the player piano works?"

"Yes, you did."

Van blew out the candles on the candelabra. He took Ariele's hand, and they walked down the hallway to the parlor. The last faint light of the setting sun shone weakly through the glass doors. From its place in the corner, the piano silently beckoned to them.

Van bent to open up the lid on the piano bench. "We'll find what we need in here," he explained.

Ariele saw that the inside of the bench was filled with rolls of paper. They reminded her of a collection of parchment scrolls she'd once viewed in an exhibit. But when Van lifted one of them out for her inspection, she noted that it bore numerous indentations.

Opening the door on the front of the piano, Van positioned the roll behind a device inside the chamber. "That's the tracker bar," he said, pointing to the device. He closed the door and pushed back the cover on the keyboard. Then he flipped a switch and the piano keys chimed out the first notes of the tune.

The melody was pretty — a waltz, Ariele decided after she'd heard a few bars. She turned to Van. "Do you know the name of it?"

" 'Lovers' Serenade.' "

Ariele shifted her eyes back to the keyboard. *He would pick a title like that,* she thought. Then she felt his hand touch her arm. "Would you care to dance?"

She was bound to look at him again. "I would, but isn't the waltz kind of old-fashioned?"

Van answered by taking her hand in his and leading her to a spot in the room where there was a bit of open space.

Ariele soon realized that whatever dance he had in mind, it wasn't a waltz. Instead, it was more a matter of him simply holding her close and leading her through a few easy steps. She had no difficulty following his lead. In fact, she enjoyed the feel of his arm fixed firmly around her waist, the gentle way his hand enfolded hers.

The Serenade ended all too quickly. "Why don't we try another?" Van suggested.

"Yes, why don't we," she agreed.

He rummaged through the rolls for a moment, then chose one. "How about Beethoven's 'Moonlight Sonata'?"

Ariele couldn't believe his selection. "That's one of my all-time favorites."

Van beamed at her. "Mine too." He rewound the Serenade and put in the new roll.

The first tentative notes of the "Moonlight Sonata" filled the room. The tune was hardly conducive to dancing, but that didn't stop Van from coming to stand behind Ariele and slipping his arms around her waist. He locked his hands in front of her, securing her in his embrace. His chin came to rest lightly on her shoulder. His breath stirred her hair. The warmth from his hands seeped through the thin barrier of her dress, into her skin, touching her on some deeper, more intimate level than even dancing with him had accomplished.

Ariele closed her eyes and gave herself up to the hauntingly romantic melody, to the sweet, searing emotions that Van's presence awakened in her. She wouldn't let herself examine the implications of those emotions. She was simply content to stay where she was, her slight form curved against Van's more substantial one.

When the melody ended, Van made no move to let her go. For now — *forever,* she thought whimsically — she wanted nothing but to be held by him. He hummed seductively into her ear, repeating the last sweet notes of the Sonata.

It seemed only natural to Ariele that she should turn to gaze into his eyes. And it seemed natural too that Van should choose that same instant to bring his mouth to hers in a kiss as passionate as the Sonata itself.

"I wish," he whispered against her mouth, "that this evening would never end."

Ariele detected no trace of the egotist about him now, no sign of the fiery disposition that appeared to be one of his dominant traits. She saw only a quality of exquisite tenderness that made her question whether he was very much like Jerod, after all.

Giddily she started to tell him that perhaps their evening together didn't have to end just yet. But for some reason she tilted her head slightly so that her eyes focused beyond Van, and what she saw froze the words in her throat before she could get them out. Framed in a pane of one of the double doors was a man's face. It was the gardener's, she knew instinctively, and he was staring straight at her. She must have stiffened, for Van held her a little away from himself.

"What is it?" he asked, sounding slightly dazed.

"Denton. In . . . one of the doors," she stammered. She looked again. The gardener's face was still there. Then suddenly it was gone.

Van released her and went to the doors. He peered out. "I don't see him."

Ariele touched the pane of glass where Denton had appeared. "Here. He was watching me . . . us." How long had the gardener stood there? Had he observed them the whole time? The thought sent a cold chill through her.

Van tried the doors; he couldn't open them.

"I locked them, remember?" Ariele undid the latch, and she and Van stepped outside together.

Ariele saw no sign of the gardener, but

then the whole lawn was filled with deep shadows. It would have been easy for him to steal away unnoticed. A gust of wind tore past the corner of the house. It set up a moaning sound through the bushes and rattled the glass on the doors. Did the wind portend another storm?

Van took firm hold of the door handles. "Come on," he said. They went back inside.

After locking the doors, Van put on a nearby lamp. In the clear light, Ariele saw that his brow was etched with lines, the corners of his mouth curved downward. "When I speak with Denton, I'll make it very plain that he's not to come anywhere near the manor in the evenings. If you see him hanging around here again, I want you to let me know immediately."

"Maybe he was just curious." Ariele wasn't sure whether she said it more to convince Van or herself. But it could be true. Hadn't Emma surprised her just the other day in the mistress's suite?

"Maybe," Van agreed, but his expression was somber as he rewound the piano roll.

Ariele watched him with a certain wistfulness, sensing that their evening together was over.

"I'd better be going for tonight," he said,

confirming her fears. Then he smiled. "We could start work on the carousel tomorrow. That is, if you want to."

"I want to."

"Tell Emma I'll have my piece of apple pie tomorrow too."

Ariele had almost forgotten that the housekeeper expected to serve them dessert in the parlor. "I will."

He switched off the lamp, plunging the room into near darkness. "Just one more thing, Ariele."

She could barely see his face. Leaning toward him, she asked, "What is it, Van?"

"Save the next dance for me." He placed a quick kiss on her lips. Then he put her arm through his and, together, they went into the hallway.

Chapter Nine

Ariele couldn't sleep. She was too keyed up from the evening she'd spent with Van, restless with memories of him holding her as the "Moonlight Sonata" played — and of the kiss they'd shared after the music stopped. Lying in the darkness of her room, she found it impossible to calm her spinning thoughts and quell her errant emotions.

She was forced to concede that what she felt for Van was more than mere attraction. But it wasn't love. It couldn't be. The very idea was ridiculous. Yet, over dinner hadn't she been given a generous glimpse beneath the tough exterior he projected? And hadn't she liked what she'd seen there?

The answers to her self-imposed questions gave Ariele little comfort. But the subject of Van wasn't the only one that interfered with her peace of mind. There was also the gardener and his shadowy appearances in and around the manor. She'd pretty well dismissed her initial encounter with him in the parlor. But tonight he had made a definite intrusion on her privacy — hers and

Van's, that was. Again, Ariele told herself not to make too much of Denton's elusiveness, that it was natural for him to want to know about the new owner of the estate. Maybe he had just been passing by outside, observed movement in the parlor, and drawn closer for a better look.

Far greater threats to her well-being than Denton, she reasoned, were the greedy horse farmer who was a suspected murderer and arsonist, a pair of sticky-fingered sisters who drove a hearse and severed telephone wires, and perhaps even the ambitious president of a local society who hoped to buy Sheldrake for a song.

With a sigh, Ariele pushed back the coverlet and got up. The moon had risen in the sky, dispelling some of the darkness outside. Its light puddled on the floor, illuminating the room so that she could make her way over to the window.

She'd opened the window when she'd come upstairs. The wind had dissipated some time ago to a refreshing breeze that gently stirred the curtains. Its coolness felt good against Ariele's cheeks as she knelt by the window.

The lawn below was plainly visible. Only Burroughs Lane, with its hedgerows, was in total blackness. Ariele easily picked out the shape of her Honda in the lane. But the car that had been parked next to it was missing. If it were Denton's, where had he gone off to so late at night?

Thinking about the gardener made Ariele uneasy all over again. She forced him out of her mind and considered her aunt instead. Had Elizabeth Sheldrake knelt by this same window, gazing out at a moonlit sky? Had the view provoked in her romantic images of the man whose picture was in the locket? Had she too been kept awake by the memory of a kiss?

Suddenly, Ariele had an urge to find out what was in the trunk in the mistress's suite. She put aside unsettling thoughts that the rooms would be dismally dark this time of night and located the ring of keys in her purse. Then she set off down the corridor.

Ariele pushed open the door to the suite and groped along the wall for a light switch. She found one and was gratified when overhead lights came on in both rooms. She went right to the trunk. As fortune would have it, the first key she tried fit the lock perfectly.

The lid of the trunk made a small groan of protest as she flung it back. Ariele's initial impression of the trunk was that it wasn't as full as she'd anticipated it would be. But that would serve to make her task less formidable.

She reached in and lifted out the several colorful swatches of cloth that lay on top. Unfolding them, she realized they were shawls. The shawls were pretty, if a bit faded.

She put them aside and went on to the next items, which were a dozen or so sets of embroidered pillowcases. Underneath the cases was an equal number of tapestries. Most were unfinished; several had rusty needles stuck in them with embroidery floss dangling from the needles' eyes.

After the tapestries came a few paintings, woodland scenes similar to the ones that were hung in the bedroom. None of them bore a signature, so Ariele had no idea who had painted them. With a sigh of disappointment, she laid the pictures beside the stack of tapestries. She was almost to the bottom of the trunk and had yet to come across anything exciting.

She brought out the last items — more pieces of cloth, this time, scarves. A large crimson one with a white fringe lay on the floor of the trunk. From the way it was folded over, Ariele guessed that something was wrapped up in the scarf. Pushing aside the satiny folds of cloth, she discovered a book.

The book, a thin volume, was bound in rich white leather. Ariele turned it over. On the cover were the initials "E.B." The gold-filigreed letters were surrounded by a design of delicate rosebuds and ivy leaves.

Ariele opened to the first page, noting the title. "*Sonnets from the Portuguese and Other Love Poems*," she read softly to herself. The sonnets were by Elizabeth Barrett Browning. Ariele loved Barrett Browning's works, and now it appeared she had another gem to add to her growing collection of books.

Turning to the next page, Ariele began to realize that this particular volume was even more valuable than she'd thought. There was a message written in a bold hand on the page. Her heart thumped wildly as she read the few lines.

"My Dearest Elizabeth,
To my heart, my very soul and breath, my reason for existence.
Do you remember the vow we made to each other at the carousel that wondrous night? When I close my eyes, I can feel the soft warmth of you in my arms still, taste the sweet wine of your kisses.

*My Darling, may our love last for eter-
nity. May we now share a lifetime of the
purest happiness a man and woman can
know together.*

*Yours Forevermore,
Thomas Montalone."*

Ariele sat back on her heels, stunned by
the intimacy of the man's words — the
man, she was certain now, whose picture
was in the locket.

She leafed through the book and made
another discovery. Pressed between two of
the pages was a dried rose. Ariele surmised
the flower came from the arbor in the
formal garden. With great care, she lifted
the delicate flower from the book and considered the poem printed there. It was entitled "That Day."

Reading the several stanzas, Ariele wondered why her aunt had chosen such a
melancholy poem. Was it because the vows
she and Thomas had made to each other
had been broken?

Ariele made a vow of her own as she laid
aside the book and packed away the
trunk's contents. She would somehow
learn the truth about Thomas and Elizabeth and the love they had shared. She
took the book again. Holding it to her

breast, she turned out the lights in the suite and hastened down the hall to her room.

As she got into bed, Ariele came to a decision. She would seek out Emma in the morning and persuade her to share whatever secrets she knew about Thomas Montalone.

On the edge of falling into a dreamy sleep, Ariele was roused by a noise. She recognized it as the sound of a car traveling up the lane. She rose from the bed and padded over to the window. Peeking out, she saw the twin beams of the headlights flash over the lawn. The car pulled to a stop beside her Honda, and a man emerged from the driver's side. It was Denton.

The gardener began to cross the grass. Instead of turning at the corner of the house toward the path, he made tracks for the front door of the manor. The breath caught in Ariele's throat. What was he doing coming this way?

He seemed to disappear when he got to the porch. Ariele leaned nearer the window in an effort to locate him. At that instant Denton stepped back into the light. He raised his head and looked toward the window. Seeing his face, Ariele ducked back. Had he spotted her?

She waited for a moment, then moved forward again. Peering down, she saw no sign of him, and she made herself believe he'd gone off to his cottage. Still, she took a last glimpse out the window. The yard appeared empty, and so she went back to bed. It wasn't until later when she was safely snuggled under the coverlet that she realized she was trembling.

Though she'd barely slept, Ariele got up early the next morning. Breakfast was again waiting for her on a tray. She ate her meal quickly, then went to search for Emma.

She found her in the downstairs parlor, dusting the furniture. The housekeeper swung around at Ariele's approach. "Did you sleep well last night, Miss Harwood?" she asked with a smile.

Ariele returned the smile. "Well enough." In her hands she held the book of sonnets and the locket with Thomas's picture inside. "I'd like to talk with you for a few minutes, Emma. It's important."

"Of course," the housekeeper replied, though her expression was guarded.

"Why don't we sit on the sofa," Ariele suggested. She sat down first. Emma followed, propping her feather duster against a nearby table. "Last night I found something interesting in my aunt's trunk."

"You've got a key to the trunk?"

"Yes. It was on a ring of keys that I discovered in my aunt's deposit box."

Emma sat erect. She looked away. "And what did you find in the trunk that was so interesting?"

"This." Ariele held up the book of sonnets for Emma to see. "It was wrapped in a scarf." She slowly opened the book to the inscription.

The housekeeper's eyes widened; she brought her hands to her face. "Oh, my dear," she cried.

"Thomas Montalone," Ariele said quietly. She snapped open the locket and laid it across the inscription, "The picture is of Thomas, isn't it? He and Elizabeth were in love, weren't they?"

Emma bowed her head. For a moment she sat silently, only moving to reach out and take the opened locket from Ariele. "Miss Sheldrake and Mr. Montalone were very much in love," she said at last, fingering the tiny photograph.

Ariele sensed the housekeeper was on the verge of telling her whatever secrets she knew about the couple. "I've seen the carousel, Emma."

178

The older woman looked astonished. "You found it too, did you? Miss Sheldrake's father had it built for her to play on." Emma returned to a study of the picture. "When she grew up, she and Mr. Montalone used to meet there."

"You knew Thomas Montalone?"

"Not directly." Emma met Ariele's eyes. "My mother was employed by Samuel Sheldrake when I was just a child. His wife had died suddenly, and he was in need of a housekeeper. I got acquainted with Elizabeth Sheldrake when I was ten. She was older — eighteen — but she took a liking to me. She would invite me to ride on the carousel, and she even taught me a bit about playing the piano." The housekeeper paused.

"Yes, go on," Ariele encouraged her.

"I guess you could say I was awestruck by her. I thought Miss Sheldrake was the most beautiful thing I'd ever seen in my life. And him . . ." She shook her head.

"You mean Thomas Montalone? You saw him?"

Emma laughed softly. "Oh, I saw him all right. I saw the two of them together at the carousel. I had known Miss Sheldrake was being courted. So one evening when she put on a pretty white dress with lace

179

around the neck, I secretly followed her." Emma sighed; her eyes took on an unfocused look. "Mr. Montalone was waiting for her at the merry-go-round. You see, behind the thicket there's an old wagon road that runs between the two estates. I imagine he was accustomed to coming that way to meet her."

Emma leaned toward Ariele. "I must tell you, Miss Harwood," she said in an intimate whisper, "at the time I considered Mr. Montalone a prince, the handsomest man I'd ever set eyes on. He wore a black velvet suit that evening. He cut such a tall, rugged figure in it, and the way his hair, all blond and wavy, gleamed in the last of the sun . . . it gave him the appearance of almost an angel."

Ariele thought of another man whose hair gleamed in the sunshine. "So Thomas Montalone was the prince, and my aunt was the princess — like in a fairy tale."

"That's how it seemed to me back then. He took her hand, and they stood staring into each other's eyes. I heard them talking, though I couldn't make out what they said. Then he put his arms around her and kissed her. And I ran away." Emma laughed again. "I guess I was afraid of getting caught, spying on them like that."

Ariele could hardly blame Emma for spying. "But what happened between them so that they never married?"

Emma's face suddenly wore a haunted expression. "There was a . . . terrible tragedy."

"What kind of a tragedy?"

"A fire. A man was killed."

The word *fire* provoked in Ariele images of Archer Winslow, and of a barn with two helpless colts trapped inside. "You mean Thomas died in a fire?"

"No. Another man who also claimed to love Miss Sheldrake. I wasn't told about it directly, though it soon became the gossip of the valley. I overheard my mother and father talking." She smiled briefly. "I used to spy on them too. I learned that there'd been a confrontation of some sort between Mr. Montalone and the other man, whose name was Jess Walker. The next thing, Jess Walker was dead."

"And people thought Thomas was responsible."

Emma nodded, her eyes shiny with tears. "Excuse me," she said, wiping at her cheeks. "It's just . . . I was very fond of Miss Sheldrake." She stopped to compose herself. "Shortly after the fire, we moved away and my mother went to work for someone else. I grew up, got married. But

181

then my husband died young, and when I heard Mr. Sheldrake had lost his second wife and was again looking for a housekeeper, I came to work for him."

Ariele reached out to touch Emma's arm. "I'm sure my aunt was very happy to have you here."

"Yes, she was. But the whole affair with the fire affected her so that she withdrew into herself. She understood that she and Mr. Montalone could never be . . . together." Emma's chin quivered. "Miss Sheldrake mourned for him the rest of her life, I expect."

"And Thomas?" Ariele presumed he too was dead.

"I suppose he's mourning still."

"He's alive?" Emma nodded. "How do you know that?"

"Because he still lives on his estate. If you were to go by way of the wagon road, you'd see it directly."

"I'd very much like to visit him, Emma."

"Ha! I wish you luck, Miss Harwood. He never receives visitors. Ever since he came back, he's stayed to himself. About the only people who have seen him are members of his family — and they've all since died — and his housekeeper."

"Was my aunt a recluse too?"

Emma took a long, last look at the picture in the locket. Then she clasped the locket shut and handed it to Ariele. "Miss Sheldrake didn't go out much," she acknowledged.

"But Mr. Caulfield came to see her, didn't he?"

"Yes, and his visits did her a world of good."

"He believes the carousel could be restored." Ariele tossed out the statement to see Emma's reaction.

The housekeeper brightened considerably. "No doubt he's right. Mr. Caulfield's a wonderful young man, and smart as they come."

The comments weren't lost on Ariele, but she wanted Emma's opinion on another person. "How about Archer Winslow? Did he visit my aunt too?"

Emma's expression turned dour. "He came, more times than I'd care to count, the last year that she lived."

"Did she welcome his visits?"

"I doubt welcome would be the right word," the housekeeper retorted. "But she was ill, and I expect Mr. Winslow has his ways about him, if you know what I mean." She shook her head. "I never liked what I saw in Mr. Winslow, if I dare say so."

You're not the only one, Ariele could have told her. "What about Zelda and Blanche? They didn't neglect their half-sister, did they?"

"Neglect? They paid more attention to her than they had the years before put together."

"Do you think the sisters could have gotten hold of keys to the manor?"

Emma's eyes narrowed. "I expect it's possible."

"Could Mr. Winslow have gotten hold of keys too?"

"Nothing would surprise me, Miss Harwood. During those last months, there was a great deal of confusion with the sisters and Mr. Winslow coming and going." Emma bit her lip. "I'm sorry. I should have taken better notice."

"Don't apologize. You couldn't have stopped them." Ariele paused. "Did Philip Hubbard ever show up?"

"Just once." Emma looked thoughtful. "He's another slick one. But he and Miss Sheldrake didn't see eye to eye about a lot of things, and I guess he was smart enough to know not to try to push her, even if he and his Society would like to turn Sheldrake into a sort of mausoleum."

Ariele smiled at Emma's choice of

words. "So you wouldn't put Philip Hubbard in quite the same category as Archer Winslow then?"

"No, I wouldn't." Emma seemed firm about the matter.

"The reason I've asked you these questions is because the other day I discovered something missing from the library. It was a small sculpture, an alabaster bust of a young girl. Maybe you know the one, Emma."

The housekeeper looked confused. "The bust's missing?"

"Yes. I hate to say this, but I strongly suspect that Zelda or Blanche took it."

But Emma appeared not to be listening. "Miss Harwood," she said, her voice high and thin, "the blue vial, the one in the mistress's suite with the rose perfume in it. You had it in your hand the other evening when I came into the suite. You took it with you, didn't you?"

"No, I didn't."

"Then it's missing too." The color drained from Emma's cheeks.

"Blanche was upstairs the other day . . . alone."

Emma started to reply, but a loud knock at the front door interrupted her. "Now who could that be?" she said, excusing herself.

Ariele felt restive, anticipating that Van

would soon come striding through the door. But he didn't appear; instead Emma returned, bearing a huge bouquet of flowers wrapped in green florist's paper.

"For you, Miss Harwood." Emma handed her the flowers.

Ariele stared at the lavish bouquet. Nestled against a background of deep green fern were pale pink tulips, white feathery daisies, lavender and gold dahlias, and delicate sprigs of baby's breath.

"Looks like you've got an admirer," Emma remarked before turning away.

An admirer. Ariele smiled to herself. Had Van enjoyed their evening together so much that he had been moved to send her flowers? She searched for a card and finally found it tucked well down in the bouquet. Her hands shook slightly as she opened it. But when she saw the signature spread across the bottom of the card, she trembled for a different reason.

The flowers weren't from Van. They were from Archer Winslow. That wasn't all. A message was written on the card. Ariele read it to herself.

"Shall I call this the proverbial olive branch, Miss Harwood, a gesture of peace and friendship? Call it whatever I might,

my fondest wish is for you to see Winslow Farms. Would tomorrow morning be convenient, say ten o'clock? If another time would be more suitable, please call 356-2299 and my housekeeper will relay your message. I await your visit with great anticipation."

Ariele made her way to the sofa and sagged onto it. Absently she laid the bouquet aside, her whole attention focused on the card she held in her hand.

"Would you like me to take these for you, Miss Harwood?"

Ariele started at the sound of Emma's voice. Springing up from the sofa, she saw the housekeeper had the bouquet of flowers in her hand. "I know just the vase for . . ."

"No!" Ariele surprised herself as much as she did Emma. "I mean . . . Emma, the flowers are from Archer."

Emma stared at the flowers now as if they were poison ivy instead.

"Please, just throw them out."

"Yes. Yes, I will, Miss Harwood." The housekeeper hurried out, holding the bouquet at arm's length.

Ariele slowly lowered herself to the sofa. What would Emma's reaction have been if she'd told her about Archer's invitation?

Now the dilemma was whether or not to accept it. If she were honest with herself, she'd have to admit that she was morbidly curious about Winslow Farms. What she'd learned about Archer from Van, and now Emma, only fueled her curiosity all the more.

She was still debating what to do when she heard the ring of the telephone in the library. She rose to answer it, but Emma apparently got there first.

The housekeeper's head poked around the doorway. "It's Mr. Caulfield for you," she announced. As soon as Ariele took the receiver in her hand, Emma discreetly departed.

Van's voice on the other end sounded far away. He was calling, he said, to let her know he wouldn't be free to work on the carousel until the next afternoon. But, he told her, he would try to stop by the manor today — if he could manage to squeeze it into his schedule. He concluded the brief conversation with an abrupt good-bye before she had time to respond to anything he'd said.

The decisive click of the receiver on the other end rang in Ariele's ears. She hung up the phone, feeling vaguely annoyed. Van hadn't made any mention of their evening together, nor given her the slightest hint that he had any memory of it. Had she acted foolishly, letting him hold her in such an intimate way?

She chided herself for being too sensitive. Besides, she had more serious matters weighing on her mind, not the least of which was Archer's invitation. Suddenly Ariele came to a decision. She would accept the invitation, visit Winslow Farms in the morning. And whether Van could manage to squeeze a moment from his busy schedule to stop by the manor was of no concern to her at all.

Chapter Ten

"So, Miss Harwood, what do you think of my farm?" Archer Winslow's mouth curved in a charming smile.

Ariele chose her answer carefully. "It's very impressive." She watched Archer's hand stroke slowly down the black mane of the colt in the stall where the three of them stood. His fingers paused to untangle a few strands of the mane that had somehow gotten twisted together. The act was a charitable one. But were those hands, so long and finely tapered, also capable of murder?

"I would have hoped your response would be a bit more enthusiastic, Miss Harwood. I'm wounded, you know."

Archer's voice sounded lightly teasing, but when Ariele looked into his eyes, she saw them sending her a different sort of signal, one that chilled her. She moved away from him as far as she could in the tiny box of a stall. All morning it had been like that, the two of them playing a game of cat and mouse. If she'd been attracted to him, she might have enjoyed the game, considered it seductive, even. But she felt nothing for Archer except a sense of mistrust.

"I'm sorry if you're disappointed," she said at last, reaching out to pet the colt along its ribs. The hairs were like silk against her palm.

"You could make amends by having lunch with me." Archer started toward her.

Ariele ducked her head from him. "I'm afraid that won't be possible. I have to leave now." She turned on her heel and went the other way around the colt.

Archer moved quickly. He planted himself between the colt and the wall, effectively blocking Ariele's exit. "I'm doubly wounded, Miss Harwood." His mouth curled in a petulant frown. "My chef is preparing a special meal for the two of us. Caesar salad. Fresh salmon, delivered just this morning on ice." He advanced on Ariele. She tried to back away, but only succeeded in colliding with the corner of the stall. "I thought we could combine business with pleasure," he went on.

Ariele made herself look at him. "We have no business to discuss, Mr. Winslow."

Archer lifted an eyebrow. "Is that so? I thought we had a great deal to discuss.

Specifically, the offer I'm prepared to make on your property. I guarantee you won't be able to secure a better offer than mine."

Ariele raised herself to the full height that her petite frame would allow. "You seem to have forgotten that I might not be interested in negotiating a deal with you — or with anyone else, for that matter. In fact, I may not be selling the estate." Where had *that* come from?

He looked aghast. "You don't mean you're keeping that old wreck of a place, do you?"

"I might . . . yes. Now, if you'll please let me by."

Archer stepped aside. But it became apparent he wasn't through with her yet. As she passed, he took hold of her arm. His grip was strong; he could hurt her if he wanted to. "Just one more thing, Miss Harwood." His eyes glistened. "I can assure you that you're going to regret your decision."

Ariele jerked loose from his grasp. "No, I don't think that I will," she said coldly. With that, she walked away from him, aware that he was watching her.

The heat of his gaze burned at her back long after she'd gone down the wide aisle of the foaling shed and into the glaring sunshine outside. It followed her across the gravel drive in front of the shed and over the grassy expanse that separated the shed from the larger barns.

Winslow Farms appeared idyllic, like an artfully contrived movie set, she thought now. She could hardly fault herself for failing to discover any trace of the illicit activities Van had hinted went on at the farm. She'd looked diligently enough for clues, particularly of the fire that had lined Archer's pockets with money. But what real chance had she had, with Archer meeting her the moment she stepped from her car and not leaving her side until she'd left him in the foaling shed?

Glancing back, Ariele saw no sign of the farm's owner, and she no longer felt as if she were being watched. She could go on by herself to the spot where her car was parked in the driveway. Or she could — what?

It took only a second for Ariele to make up her mind. She turned on her heel and headed in the opposite direction, away from her car. She had no plan, but she was alone at last, and it was possible she might happen upon something that hadn't been included in Archer's "tour package." But what if one of his employees stopped her, asked her what she was doing? She would feign confusion, she decided, and tell them she was lost.

No one bothered her. And as it turned out, she didn't have to go far to find what she'd been searching for. On the other side of the stables, beside a pasture, she discovered the concrete base of a building. In contrast to the lush areas of lawn that surrounded the barns, the ground here was mostly bare, with only occasional tufts of grass or small patches of weeds growing near the perimeter of the slab. Was that because a fire had consumed both the structure and the vegetation around it?

Ariele stooped down to inspect a corner of the base. She could easily picture the foaling shed that no doubt had once stood there. Now the peaceful scene, the bucolic pasture nearby where several stallions were contentedly grazing, belied the gruesome deed that had been committed at Winslow Farms one dark night a year ago.

A sound caused Ariele to look up. Had someone approached? Looking around, she saw no sign of anyone. But she decided it would be wise to go. She rose and, turning in the other direction, headed for the driveway. She didn't slow her pace or glance behind her until she'd made it safely to the refuge of her car.

When Ariele pulled into the lane at Sheldrake a few minutes later, she saw that Denton's car was gone. In its place was a battered red pickup truck. *Now who,* she wondered as she got out of her Honda.

Emma met her in the foyer. "Mr. Caulfield's here," the housekeeper said at once. She sounded eager. "That is, he's at the carousel. He came right after you left this morning. Said I should be sure and tell you as soon as you got home."

"Thank you, Emma," she said absently. So the pickup in the driveway was Van's. She hadn't thought of him as owning any other form of transportation but The Litigator. What was he doing here? Hadn't he told her on the phone that he couldn't get away until the afternoon?

The housekeeper shot her a quizzical glance. "It seemed to me Mr. Caulfield was a bit disappointed that you weren't home."

"Yes . . . well . . ." Ariele looked away. She hadn't told either Emma or Van of her plans for the morning. And she wasn't in a mood now to divulge the disturbing details of her visit to Winslow Farms.

Emma went on, "I've made sandwiches

for lunch. Thought I might put them in a hamper along with a thermos of iced tea. If you like, you could take them out to Mr. Caulfield and the two of you could have a picnic."

Emma's helpfulness made Ariele smile. "That sounds tempting. I just need a couple of minutes to freshen up."

The housekeeper nodded. "Come by the kitchen when you're finished. I'll have everything ready for you."

Ariele spotted Van before he saw her. Approaching the carousel, she was rather shocked to see a rather large opening in the thicket that hadn't been there on her last trip. She had a clear view of Van perched on a short ladder beside the carousel. He had a hammer in one hand; his other hand was stretched up, as if he were reaching for something under the roof.

Dressed casually today in jeans and a white T-shirt, he more resembled a construction worker than a lawyer. Ariele recalled that he'd been both. And she was compelled to notice that the jeans fit him every bit as snugly as his leather pants did.

He must have known she was there, for he turned just as she was about to call to him. His face broke into a smile. "Hi," he said, climbing off the ladder to meet her. His eyes studied her face so thoroughly that Ariele's cheeks began to flush. Then his attention focused on the basket in her hands. "What do you have there?"

"It's supposed to be sandwiches and iced tea," she replied with a smile. "But from the feel of the basket, I'd say it's more like a full-fledged picnic."

"This is Emma's doing, I assume." Van took the basket from her and set it on the ground. Then he clasped her hands in his. "I missed you," he said softly.

Gone was any trace of the formality he'd displayed on the phone. Ariele's heart did a little flip. "I missed you too," she admitted. She felt the tension begin to lift from her, like a weight. She hadn't realized until now how much strain she'd been under that morning.

Still, Van must have sensed her uneasiness. His hands squeezed hers. "Is something wrong?" he asked.

Ariele stiffened. A part of her wanted to tell him about her visit to Winslow Farms. Another part resisted — and won. "No. I'm just surprised that you're here. The truck fooled me."

Van grinned. "The Litigator isn't very handy for hauling tools around, I'm afraid."

"No, I don't imagine it is. But shouldn't you be working?"

"I am working. Actually, court proceedings for the case I'm prosecuting were called off for today — and for the next two weeks. The defendant had to be rushed from the jail to the hospital last night."

"That sounds serious."

Van nodded. "A minor heart attack." He paused. "What that means for us is that I should be able to swing taking the afternoons off and spending them here." He looked for her reaction.

Ariele couldn't hide her pleasure at the news. "That's wonderful." And wonderful too was the feeling of his fingers wrapped securely around hers. "I notice you've already cleared a path to the merry-go-round. What else have you accomplished?"

"I'll show you." He released her and led her over to the ladder. "This." He made a gesture toward the carousel.

Ariele saw that three tall wooden pillars were wedged between the roof and the floor.

"I thought I'd better shore up the roof before it collapses on our heads," he explained.

Ariele was impressed. "You did all this yourself?"

"Not quite. I enlisted Denton's help."

"Oh." Denton was another subject that she wasn't entirely comfortable with. Her expression must have given her away.

"Don't worry," Van said. "I let Denton know in no uncertain terms that he wasn't to go near the manor anymore, except to pick up something from Emma in the kitchen. And then he's to use the back door only." He stared at her thoughtfully. "Ariele, I want you to have the locks changed on the doors of the manor."

She wondered at Van's sudden insistence. When he'd mentioned the subject before, he'd only recommended changing the locks. Did he view Denton as creepy too? "Because of Denton?" she asked.

"Because I don't want any more strange activities going on. And because I don't want to lie awake nights worrying about your safety."

He was worried about her safety? If he were only aware of the things Archer had said to her in the foaling shed, the danger signals his eyes had flashed her way. "All right," she agreed, relieved herself at the idea of getting new locks on the doors. Now she wouldn't have to be concerned about the Pilchard sisters or Archer gaining entry to the manor with a key.

"I know of a good locksmith. If you'd like, I can arrange for him to come out tomorrow," Van offered.

"Yes, why don't you do that."

Van grew contemplative for a moment, and she wondered again what he was thinking. "Are you going to give me a job to do?" she asked at last. "Or shall we eat first?"

His hand came up to brush back a strand of her hair. "I'd rather hold you in my arms," he confessed. "But I suppose we'd better eat to keep up our strength for . . . working." He chuckled at Ariele's blushing response. Then he retrieved the basket, and they found a place on the ground where they could sit in relative comfort.

Unpacking the basket, Ariele discovered that her suspicions had been right. Emma had provided them with a veritable feast. Besides the sandwiches and tea, the housekeeper had packed oranges, wedges of cheese, and huge pieces of the apple pie that hadn't been eaten the night before. She'd even provided a blanket for them to sit on. Ariele arranged the blanket on the ground.

Over their lunch, Ariele had the opportunity to tell Van what she'd learned about the man whose picture was in her aunt's locket. She told him of her discovery of the book of sonnets and quoted Thomas's inscription as accurately as her memory would allow.

"I knew there was something special about this place," Van said, regarding her over his sandwich.

"Yes." Ariele thought of Emma's vivid description of the young lovers meeting at the carousel. It was obvious to her that there was a sort of magic at work when she and Van were here as well — a magic that sparked encounters of the romantic kind.

Though the subject was one she could easily consider all day, Ariele was determined to steer the conversation in a more practical vein. So she asked Van about his practice. He warmed to the subject, and she learned that he had recently been appointed prosecuting attorney for the county. She saw his enthusiasm for the position. At her prompting, he briefly related a few of the more colorful cases he'd prosecuted, including his latest one in which the crime was the kidnapping of a prize sow and her twelve piglets.

"I assume it was a happy ending for the pigs."

Van laughed. "Very happy since the defendant didn't have a particularly brilliant criminal mind. The best part of all was when the bailiff tried to lead the sow up to the stand. Talk about a reluctant witness. . . ."

Ariele giggled, picturing the scene. But Van grew introspective again, and she wondered if he was recalling another case, one he hadn't been able to prosecute because the defendant had never been brought to trial — the case of Archer Winslow, suspected murderer and arsonist.

When they were finished eating, Van packed the few leftovers away in the basket. Ariele took the blanket and shook it out. Without warning, Van caught the loose corners of the blanket, nearly snatching the cover away from her. "I'll help you," he said. Their hands met where they brought the corners together, and they stood, with the blanket between them, gazing at each other. All at once Van tossed the blanket aside. Whispering her name, he took Ariele's face in his hands and kissed her.

When their lips finally parted, Ariele expelled a shaky breath. "I believe you were going to give me a job," she said, though her thoughts were not at all on work at the moment.

Van sighed. "You're right, but the temptation is great to just ask you to kiss me every ten minutes or so. That should be inspiration enough for me to do the jobs of two people."

She laughed, and that seemed to serve to bring them back to the subject at hand. Van asked her, "Would you like me to show you how to give a wooden horse a new coat of paint?"

"I'd like that very much," she said, reaching up to place a surprise kiss on his chin.

The locksmith came the next morning and installed sturdy new deadlocks on both the front and back doors of the manor. Ariele had to smile a little at Van's expediency, but she was also happy to have the added security. Now she could focus her attention more fully on the work they had begun on the carousel.

Ariele soon discovered, much to her astonishment, that she seemed to possess a talent for restoring wooden horses. After Van had taken down one of the animals from its post and shown her how to strip off the old paint and prepare the bare wood for a fresh coat, she'd found she could work on her own while he started repairs on the merry-go-round floor.

Over their first weekend on the project,

they saw visible signs of progress. By dusk on Sunday, Van had replaced almost half of the old floor with new boards that he and Ariele had carried between them from the truck to the carousel. And Ariele had successfully removed all of the old paint from the horse. They both agreed the animal should be restored to its original color of white with pink and blue trim.

Leaving the carousel that evening, Ariele couldn't remember when she'd enjoyed herself so much. For the first time in ages she was content to live her life moment by moment, thinking only as far ahead as the completion of the restoration project. Even the task of inventorying her books had taken a backseat to working on the merry-go-round.

She'd managed to convince herself it wasn't healthy to look too far into the future — either Sheldrake's or her own. If she did, she'd have to remind herself that the only sane course for her to take was to sell the estate and leave Burroughs County and Cyril Vance Caulfield III behind forever.

Beside her, Van reached for her hand. She didn't resist. She couldn't; she thrived on his attention. But she didn't want to think about that, either.

They came to the bench and rose arbor. "Let's sit down for a minute," Van suggested.

They sat. In the deepening dusk, a lone bird sang a subdued song. The roses on the arbor took on a darker shade of red; one caught a fading ray of the sun, glowing like an ember in the soft light. Van broke off the bloom and removed the thorns from its stem. He looked at Ariele. "Bend your head a little," he said. She obeyed and he placed the rose in her hair.

As they looked at each other, Ariele couldn't help thinking, *This is how it must have been for Thomas and Elizabeth.*

Then suddenly, Van's attention was diverted elsewhere. Ariele turned to see what had caught his eye. "Oh," she breathed. Not five feet away from them, perched on a leaf, was one of the loveliest butterflies she had ever seen. The velvet green of the leaf provided the perfect backdrop to show off the vivid orange-and-black markings of the butterfly.

"Don't move," Van said quietly from right behind her.

"I won't," she whispered.

"Isn't he beautiful?"

"Yes, he is." She recalled another conversation they'd had about a butterfly. Though she'd wanted to deny it, she'd been irresistibly drawn to Van even then.

"He's called a fritillary."

Ariele almost looked back at Van. "A . . . ?"

He laughed quietly. "A fritillary. A great spangled, to be exact."

Ariele felt his hand lift the hair from her neck. His breath caressed her skin. She tried to stay focused on the butterfly, but Van's touch was making her giddy. "How do you . . . know so much about butterflies?" she said with a little gasp.

His lips sought her ear and kissed it. "They're a hobby of mine. I photograph them."

She could have sworn he had another hobby. "The picture of the butterfly in your office." *The one that's the color of your eyes,* she might have added. "Didn't you say he's found only in Hawaii?"

"Yes. I photographed him on Oahu. Ariele . . ." He took her by the shoulders and turned her away from the butterfly to face him.

Though the butterfly had been gorgeous to look at, Ariele found this new view even more satisfying. "What?"

"I would love to have you with me when I take my next trip. I'll be tracking down the lilac-banded longtail in Argentina."

"The . . . lilac-banded longtail . . . in Argentina?" she repeated. It sounded fascinating. But was this something he told every woman he found attractive? "Van, I . . ."

He touched her mouth with his thumb, silencing her. "You don't need to say anything. I can feel your uncertainty. But there is something you need to know." He framed her face in his hands, burying his fingers in the thick curls of her hair. "I'm falling in love with you, Ariele," he whispered. His thumb moved slowly across her lips. Then all she knew was the heady taste of him as his mouth took hers in a fervent kiss.

Finally, she tore herself from him. Awash in the emotions stirred up by his kiss, his declaration of love for her, Ariele found it impossible to think. But she discovered she had no need for rational thought. What Van said next spoke to her heart, and she let it sort out the meaning of his words.

"Don't deny what you're feeling," he said. "Don't fear what you know is the truth." He shook his head. "I've questioned myself too. But the only conclusion I've been able to come to is that I've never been more sure of anything in my life than I am of my love for you."

His words chimed in her ears and sent a

flood of warmth rushing through her. But why did he believe she was fearful of loving him? "I'm not afraid of the truth, Van."

"I'm glad to hear that," he said quietly. He got up from the bench, bringing her with him. "Now, what I really started to say a little while ago is, will you have dinner out with me? I know a place that's informal, quiet." He smiled sheepishly at her. "I hope you'll say yes because I already told Emma she should take the night off."

A small knot of uneasiness formed in Ariele's stomach. "Will we be taking your truck or . . . The Litigator?" She posed the question as casually as possible.

"Well, the truck's here, though I admit it's not a very glamorous mode of transportation." He looked thoughtful for a moment. "Would you rather ride on my motorcycle?"

"No . . . no, the truck's fine. In fact . . . I'd rather go in the truck," she stammered. She turned from him and began walking again.

Van caught up with her. He touched her arm. "So that's it. You have an aversion to motorcycles, don't you?"

"Why do you say that?" she retorted, her gaze fixed straight ahead.

"Because that's the way you're acting." His voice carried an edge. "Don't you trust me with your safety, Ariele?"

"That's a ridiculous question," she snapped. *Wasn't it?* "Of course I trust you."

This time he stopped her. Putting his hands on her shoulders, he made her face him. "Then prove it by letting me take you tonight on The Litigator."

His softly spoken challenge brought Ariele to the point of tears. Did he think he could use his charm to make her do his bidding? He really was no better than Jerod, after all! "I don't have to prove anything to you or . . . or to anybody." She meant to sound in command, but her voice quavered.

"Ariele." He reached for her.

"No, don't." She pulled away from him.

"I'm sorry, Ariele." He looked genuinely contrite. "Can you tell me what happened?"

She saw there was no further use in pretending. When he held out his arms to her, she willingly went into them. "I was involved with someone. We were on his motorcycle and he . . ." In that instant the whole horrifying sequence of events flashed through her mind. She saw the sharp bend in the road looming ahead; Jerod leaning the bike into the curve at warp speed; herself, arms clutched around his waist, screaming at him to stop; him laughing derisively at her; the sickening squeal of the tires, the stench of spent rubber; the wild fish-tailing of the bike as Jerod finally lost all control of it.

"Tell me," she heard Van urge her.

But all she could say was, "His recklessness almost got us both killed."

"The man was an idiot and a fool!" Van's voice was sharp with anger, but there was a tremor in it too. He lifted Ariele's chin so that her eyes met his. She'd never seen such a look of pure protectiveness in another's gaze before. "When I talked about risks the other night, I did not mean the kind that would endanger the woman that I love — or myself or anyone else, for that matter. Ariele, believe me, I play it very safe when I'm on The Litigator. And when I'm behind the wheel of my truck, for that matter."

Ariele closed her eyes briefly. "I believe you," she said. She did. And she was finally able to lay to rest the comparisons she'd been making between the man whose arms were entwined around her and the one who had nearly ended her life.

Van moved her back from himself. "Now that that's settled and we're taking the truck, you have an important decision to make." He smiled. "Are you hungry for steak or seafood or Italian or . . ."

Chapter Eleven

The next morning Ariele awoke to a phone call from Van. He sounded exceptionally cheerful. She felt no less happy herself. After all, hadn't they enjoyed each other's company immensely the evening before? And when he'd left her at the front door of the manor at midnight, hadn't his kisses and caresses shown her how much he'd hated leaving her, even for a few hours? Had he phoned just to say that he missed her?

"I can tell you're in a good mood this morning, Ariele."

"I am. I assume you are too."

"An exceptionally good mood." He paused. "And in about an hour you're going to feel even better."

Did that mean he was coming out to the estate? "Oh? Why is that?"

"Because at ten o'clock you're going to see a hearse rambling down Burroughs Lane to the manor."

"A hearse? You mean Zelda and Blanche are coming to ransack Sheldrake again? How is that going to heighten my mood?"

"You'll see." He rang off before she had a chance to question him more on the subject.

Ariele stood for a moment, the receiver in her hand. Whatever he was up to, she had an odd feeling it had to do with Spode china.

Promptly at ten she was in the foyer, watching as the sisters' hearse creaked to a stop at the end of the drive. The Litigator was right behind the hearse.

Van got off his motorcycle and the sisters emerged from their vehicle. He went over to them briefly. Then he came across the lawn to the front door. Ariele greeted him with a smile. "I see that Zelda and Blanche have a proper escort today."

"I don't know about the proper part," Van said with a grin. He bent and brushed his mouth across her parted lips.

The brief contact was more than enough to fan the flames that the mere sight of him kindled in her these days. "Mmm. My mood's improving already," she admitted to him. But her attention was quickly diverted back to Zelda and Blanche.

The sisters were now standing at the rear of the hearse. Zelda reached into the interior of the vehicle and brought out a box. She handed the box to Blanche and took out another for herself. Then the pair labored across the lawn with their loads.

"Right this way, ladies," Van said when the sisters reached the front door. "Watch your step now."

Ariele suppressed a giggle. Van looked at her and winked. The sisters were huffing and puffing, but Zelda still managed to throw a withering glance Ariele's way and sniff loudly as she passed through the foyer. Blanche glared at Ariele, but the corners of her mouth wilted depressingly. Without a word, the sisters trooped single file down the hallway. Ariele didn't have to guess their destination.

"Come on," Van invited her. They followed Zelda and Blanche to the room with the cabinets lining the walls.

"Allow me to get the door for you, ladies." Van stepped in front of them and pushed the door open wide.

Zelda stomped across the room to the empty cabinet. She appeared about to drop her box on the floor when Van called out, "Carefully, please, Miss Pilchard." She reared her head in the air and sniffed again. But she obeyed his orders, lowering the box in a cautious manner.

Blanche mimicked her sister, except that she groaned loudly when she deposited her load. As the sisters stalked out, Blanche tossed an accusatory glance Van's way.

"I can't stand it." Ariele began to laugh. She muffled the sound by pressing her face against the sleeve of Van's shirt.

He chuckled. "A pretty sweet victory, isn't it?"

Ariele managed to compose herself. "Yes, sweet," she agreed. "But how did you do it? Twist their arms behind their backs?"

"No, but that's a pleasant thought," he said agreeably. "What I did was persuade their lawyer that it would be in their best interests to return the Spode."

"In other words, if they wanted the family jewels, then they had to part with the family china — which didn't rightfully belong to them anyway."

"You've got it." He reached in his pocket and brought out a key. "This is for you," he said, placing the key in Ariele's hand. "It's to this room — and it's the only key Zelda owned up to having. She claimed that Elizabeth gave it to her."

Ariele regarded the key, then Van. "That's interesting, if not very believable. But the sisters do have more boxes of china to cart in, don't they?"

"At least several." Van's arm slipped around her waist.

"And we're going to watch and make sure they deliver all the boxes safely, aren't we?" She could easily stay where she was the rest of the day if it meant having his arm around her.

"It would be wise, don't you agree?"

"Very wise, but will they unpack the boxes too?"

"I'm not certain I trust them that far. Maybe we'd better let Emma do the honors."

"I imagine she'll be delighted with the task."

Van's mouth skimmed her hair. "I'm sure of it."

Though she knew the sisters could return at any moment, Ariele nestled closer to Van. "I suppose you'll have to go back to town when the sisters are done."

"No. As a matter of fact, I can take the whole afternoon off to work on the carousel, though I'll need to go home and change clothes. I hope to make sizable progress today on the installation of the new floor."

"And I might get near to finishing my horse too."

"You're doing some great work."

"Thanks," she murmured.

"You're welcome." Van's gaze shifted

and focused on her lips. He cupped her chin in his hand and began to lower his mouth to hers.

A pitiful moan came from outside in the hallway. With a whispered, "Later," Van released Ariele. Their heads turned toward the door, and they had the enjoyment of watching Zelda and Blanche totter over the threshold with two more boxes of china.

On Wednesday morning Van brought Philip Hubbard out to the estate to pick up the items bequeathed to the Historical Society.

With Van in charge of the removal of the inkwells and walnut curio cabinet, Ariele decided her time would be better spent in the library. She was in the midst of sorting through a set of dusty encyclopedias when she heard a man's voice say, "Miss Harwood?" She looked up to see Philip Hubbard's face peeking around the door.

"I'm sorry to bother you, Miss Harwood," he went on, "but I wonder if I could speak with you for a moment."

Ariele got up from where she was sitting on the floor. She met Philip Hubbard in the middle of the room. He looked just as disheveled as he had the day of the reading of the will. "I have a couple of minutes," she said cautiously, not sure she cared to spend them with him.

Philip Hubbard's cheeks turned ruddy. "I want to set up an appointment with you, Miss Harwood. It's about your estate. If I may tell you this, the Historical Society has a keen interest in the manor, and we would like to get our bid in first for your property."

"Bid? You assume that I'm selling the estate?"

The flush in his cheeks spread over his face. "Aren't you?"

"Maybe not. I'm considering keeping Sheldrake."

His jaw dropped; his eyes widened. He didn't speak for a little. Clearing his throat, he said at last, "Forgive me for saying this, Miss Harwood, but I believe you'll be making a serious mistake if you don't put the manor up for sale."

"Why would it be a mistake?"

Before Philip Hubbard could reply, Van came into the room.

"What are you doing in here, Philip?"

Ariele thought that Philip looked like the proverbial cat who had gotten caught lapping up the cream. "I was just speaking with Miss Harwood."

Van folded his arms across his chest. "I

would suggest that you do that another time. I have to be back at my office in half an hour, and you still need to remove the curio cabinet."

Philip's shoulders slumped; he heaved a sigh. "All right." Addressing Ariele, he said, "I'll contact you again. You can count on that." Then he turned and went ahead of Van out of the library.

Ariele watched after the men, wondering just how persistent Philip Hubbard intended to be about buying her estate. She'd easily stood up to him today. But did he plan on pestering her if she resisted his overtures? She sincerely hoped not. She already had enough trouble with the Pilchard sisters and Archer Winslow.

As Ariele stroked her paintbrush across the horse and Van hammered a board in place, they discussed the subject of Philip Hubbard and his society's desire to lay claim to her estate.

"I really wouldn't worry too much," Van told her. "I hardly think Philip will try anything vicious." He put down his hammer and regarded her silently. "You actually told him that you might not sell?"

Somehow, as she'd related the incident to Van, the words had slipped out. Of course, he would pick up on them. She didn't answer at once, just continued with her painting. "I did say that," she conceded at last. For a moment she concentrated on feathering in a delicate detail on the bridle. Finally, she set aside her brush. "From the beginning, when I learned I'd inherited Sheldrake, my intention was to sell. But lately I've been thinking over the things you've said, and I suppose it's true that there are possibilities for the manor besides selling."

To her surprise Van offered no comment, only stared reflectively at her until at last she turned back to her work. Neither of them mentioned the subject again.

By the time she and Van left the carousel, she'd completed painting the horse and Van had gotten the new floor laid. Her accomplishment gave her a sense of satisfaction that she hadn't known apart from her job in a long time. She saw in herself a reawakened sense of adventure, and though it frightened her a little, she was forced to acknowledge that she'd never felt happier than she did here, working side by side with Van.

Where it would lead she wasn't certain. Van had declared his love for her. But did love to him mean commitment? Or did it mean he loved her until he grew tired of her or until another woman came along who caught his fancy? How many other women had he said those three words to?

Once again, Ariele told herself not to look too far ahead. It was still a couple of months until September. She could put the estate up for sale tomorrow, if she chose, and be back in Providence in time for the fall semester. For now, she had another evening with Van to anticipate. Emma was cooking dinner for them. Afterward, they would attend the late show at the town's one theater. Tonight's film was a vintage Tracy/Hepburn movie.

When they came into the manor, Emma called Ariele aside. "I'm afraid something's come up, Miss Harwood." The housekeeper looked uncertain.

"What's wrong, Emma?"

"I got a call from my sister — the one I go to every other weekend. I'm afraid it's some bad news. She twisted her ankle and needs me to come help her for a week or so. She's got someone to stay with her tonight, but tomorrow night . . ." Her hands plucked at the corners of her apron.

Ariele touched the housekeeper's hand. "Don't worry. You can stay a week or longer, if it's necessary. I'll be fine." All at once she realized that she sounded like someone who was very much in charge of her household.

"Thank you." Emma hesitated. "I'm sure by now you know that the gardener will be gone over the weekend too."

"I . . . no, he hadn't mentioned it."

"He says he's got family in the Finger Lakes area. He's used to having the weekend off, but this time he's planning on leaving early. Tomorrow afternoon, in fact. He's got quite a drive ahead of him."

Ariele couldn't say she was sorry to hear the gardener wouldn't be around for a few days. "That's no problem. He can go whenever he likes."

"I'll put some sliced meat in the refrigerator for sandwiches. I can also make you a fruit salad and a couple of casseroles that you can heat up."

"That's nice of you, Emma, but you won't need to make the casseroles. I'm sure I can find enough food to fix something for myself." Though she was by no means a gourmet cook, Ariele didn't consider herself a novice, either. And she could as easily cook a meal for two as for one — should she decide to invite a certain attorney for dinner tomorrow.

As if she'd read Ariele's mind, Emma

said in a lowered voice, "I don't know if he's told you or not, but Mr. Caulfield's favorite dish is lasagna."

The next day started out bright and sunny, but by afternoon a bank of clouds filled the western sky. The rain began before Ariele and Van had gotten all their tools put away. Van had thought to bring a tarp, which they used to cover their tools and as much of the carousel as they could.

The rain was more of a drizzle at first. As she and Van walked slowly through the mist back to the manor, Ariele enjoyed the refreshing feel of the cool drops on her face. "I love when it rains."

"I do too," Van said softly as he captured her hand in his.

They reached the manor just as the deluge began. Ariele baked the lasagna she had prepared earlier in the day. Then she and Van ate in the dining room by candlelight while the rain beat against the windowpanes.

Van smiled at her over a forkful of lasagna. "How did you know this is my favorite food?"

"Don't all men love lasagna?" she teased, though she suspected he knew Emma had told her.

They were almost finished with their

meal when a loud beeping noise interrupted their conversation.

"My pager," Van said. He looked slightly annoyed as he pulled the device from his pocket.

Ariele regarded him. "I didn't know you carried one."

"I don't always." He got up from his chair. "I'm afraid I'll have to call in. I left my portable phone at home, so I'll have to use the phone in the library."

Ariele watched him go. The dining room seemed suddenly empty and too quiet without him there.

"I'm sorry," he said when he returned. "The call was about a potential witness in a case that's coming up soon. I'm going to have to interview him tomorrow." He paused. "The problem is that he lives in Syracuse."

"Syracuse is pretty far from Larkspur, isn't it?"

"A couple hundred miles or so." Van frowned. "I hate to do this, but I'd probably better leave after dinner. I'll need to get an early start in the morning."

"Of course," she agreed, but a small stab of disappointment went through her just the same.

They finished eating. Van helped her

carry the dishes to the kitchen and load them into the dishwasher. Then Ariele walked him to the door.

Van took her in his arms. "You'll be all right alone here tonight?"

"I'll be fine."

"The doors in the parlor are locked?"

"Locked tight."

He pulled her closer. "I don't know what time I'll be back tomorrow. It might not be until evening."

"Will you come over at all then?"

"Yes. That is, if you want me to."

"I want you to."

"Good." He slipped one hand behind her head and drew her face to his. After kissing her, he said, "We'll go out for dinner tomorrow night. I want to take you someplace special."

She could have told him that any place was special to her when he was with her. "I'll look forward to it." She smiled. "Be careful."

Van left, running out to his truck through the pouring rain. Ariele wandered back through the manor to the kitchen. She set the cycle on the dishwasher. The rest of the cleanup could wait until morning. All she was in the mood for now was to curl up in bed with a book.

For good measure, she rechecked the back and front doors to make sure they were bolted. Then she tested the glass doors in the parlor. When she was satisfied everything was secure, she went upstairs.

She wasn't afraid to stay alone, was she? She told herself there was nothing to be afraid of. Just the same, she caught herself glancing over her shoulder as she passed through the hallway to her room. And before she got into bed, she switched off the lamp and looked out on the lawn below. There was nothing to be seen except for the rain streaking the window, so she put the lamp on again and took the Tennyson volume to bed with her.

Halfway through the poem "Locksley Hall" she grew so drowsy that she had to lay the book down. After turning out the lamp, she fell asleep to the sound of the rain softly pelting the windows.

Ariele woke suddenly, not to the comforting patter of the rain, but to an entirely different sound. It was a tune — a march. She'd dreamed it, of course. The march had been part of some bizarre nightmare that had caused her to wake with her heart racing.

In her dazed state, she couldn't remember details of the dream. She only knew it had been frightening — and that the march still played on in her head. But the dream was over now. Then how could she be hearing the tune? The confusion cleared, and Ariele understood that the march wasn't playing in her head at all. It was coming from inside the manor. *From the piano,* she realized with horror.

She sprang out of bed and sped into the hallway. But what she saw there made her come to an abrupt stop. The corridor was pitch-black. Had it stormed while she was asleep, causing the electricity to go out? But if the electricity was off, the piano wouldn't be playing. *That meant someone had killed the lights on purpose.*

Ariele began to move along the hallway, feeling her way with her hand. How could anyone have gotten in when all the doors were locked? Had a window been broken to gain entrance?

Ariele came to the top of the stairs. Who knew about the piano? There was Van, of course. And there was Zelda and Blanche Pilchard. Zelda had inherited the piano — and insisted on giving it to Ariele. *"I hope you'll gain much enjoyment from it,"* she'd said.

Ariele found the banister with her hand and started cautiously down the steps.

Who except Zelda would pull a trick like this? Besides, Zelda had the perfect motive — revenge for having to return the Spode.

More angry than afraid now, Ariele groped her way toward the bottom of the steps. Above the frantic pace of the march she heard the howling of the wind outside. Then suddenly she saw something in front of her. It loomed tall and white, like an apparition, and it appeared to dance wildly in time to the music.

Ariele screamed; her foot missed a step and she nearly pitched forward. She clutched at the banister. But it was too late. She'd been caught by Zelda Pilchard's bony arms.

Ariele fought to get away. "No!" she yelled angrily. It was as if she were wrestling with a ghost. There was no flesh and bone for her to grasp hold of, nothing but damp heavy cloth that whipped at her face and hands.

At last she caught a fold of material in her fingers. At the same instant the march came to its end, and Ariele suddenly discerned that what she'd been fighting wasn't a person at all, but the curtain that draped the window at the bottom of the staircase.

Feeling the absolute fool, Ariele extricated herself from the soggy curtain. In the quiet she heard the wind again and felt a cool rush of air hit her face. She saw that the window was standing wide open.

Ariele looked out. The rain seemed to have stopped. A fine thread of moonlight wove its way through a break in the clouds; it wasn't enough to illuminate the yard. Ariele considered that if Zelda had come through the window to commit her mischief, she would be long gone by now. She closed the window, then at once regretted her hasty action. Had she destroyed valuable evidence by touching the window?

Sheer logic told her she should immediately call the sheriff's office. But she remembered what Van had said about Zelda and Blanche and their contributions to the Sheriff's Benevolent Society, and she decided it would be best to talk with Van first about what had happened.

As much as she longed to investigate the parlor, Aricle forced herself to stay away. She didn't want to disturb any clues the intruder might have left there. She did try to reach the top of the windowsill to see if it had a latch; her hand didn't stretch far enough. She attempted to reassure herself that no one would crawl through the window again that night, but she wasn't entirely convinced.

Though she was still badly shaken, she made herself go back up the stairs. When she got to her room, the first thing she did was check the phone. The steady hum of the clear signal met her ears. It was the sweetest sound she'd heard recently.

Ariele stayed near the phone for several minutes, wondering what to do next. Should she try to barricade herself in? About the only thing she was strong enough to move was a chair that stood by the dresser. If someone was determined to break into the room, a chair would hardly stop them. But, to make herself feel better, she took the chair and wedged it as best she could under the doorknob. Then she went and knelt by the window.

Ariele remained there the rest of the night, scanning the yard below with her eyes. When the gray light of dawn finally crept across the grass, she went to bed and fell into a fitful sleep.

Chapter Twelve

Ariele woke around noon. Her eyes automatically went to the door to see if the chair was wedged under the knob. It was. That meant she had definitely not dreamed the strange events of the night before.

Sighing, she lay back against the pillow. What would she do with herself for the rest of the day until Van came? She'd already determined that she would stay away from the downstairs parlor so that she wouldn't chance destroying any evidence the intruder might have left behind. And she was not inclined to sort through the shelves of books in the library. The kitchen had to be cleaned up, but that shouldn't take long.

Van had said he wanted to take her someplace special for dinner. After what she had to tell him, she doubted either of them would be in the mood to eat anything. More likely, they would be calling the sheriff's office to report a break-in at the manor.

Finally, Ariele made herself get out of bed. She went to the window. Clouds still lingered in the sky and the air smelled heavy with moisture, signs that the rain might not be over yet. Turning to the closet, she selected a clean pair of jeans and a blouse. Just as she started to put the jeans on, the telephone rang. Could Van be calling her on his cellular phone? Ariele dropped the jeans and picked up the receiver.

A woman's voice came on the line asking for Emma. Ariele informed her that Emma was gone and wouldn't return for a week. In that case, the woman said, she would like to leave a message.

Ariele grabbed her purse to search for a pen and piece of paper. She located a pen with no trouble. But none of the tiny shreds of paper she pulled out were big enough to write a message on. "Could you hold for a moment?" she asked the woman.

She searched the drawers of the chest, but came up empty-handed. *This is ridiculous,* she thought. Then she remembered the desk in the mistress's suite. Surely the desk would yield a note pad or sheet of paper to write on.

Dislodging the chair from under the doorknob, Ariele hurried down the hall to the suite. When she opened the top drawer of the desk, she found a long white envelope. It would do. She grabbed it and ran back to the phone.

The message concerned an order Emma had placed at the Larkspur Mercantile Company. After she hung up, Ariele reread the message to see if she'd gotten it correct. Idly turning the envelope over in her hands, she noticed a piece of paper folded inside of it. It was not ordinary paper, she realized as she took out the sheet, but fine vellum, the kind used for correspondence.

Ariele unfolded the sheet. What was written on it was indeed a letter, one she knew at once had been written by her aunt, though it was unsigned.

"*Dearest Thomas*," the letter began. "*How can I ever find the words to tell you all the things that I have kept so long in my heart?*"

The salutation and the first line were enough to show Ariele that this was no ordinary correspondence, but a love letter. Though she knew it had been meant for Thomas's eyes only, she read on. Tears spilled down her cheeks at the regret and longing evident in each word, the sorrow woven into every line. The letter came to an abrupt, inconclusive end, and Ariele surmised that her aunt had become too ill to finish the missive she had written to the man she'd so adored.

Ariele came to a decision. She would go to the Montalone estate and attempt to deliver the letter personally to Thomas. What better use could she make of her time than that? If the older man refused to see her, she would have to entrust the letter to his housekeeper.

She retrieved the book of sonnets and placed the letter in beside the pressed rose. Then she quickly got dressed and went downstairs. For a moment she considered taking the wagon road that Emma had mentioned. The walk would undoubtedly do her good. But another glance at the sky persuaded her that it would be more prudent to drive to the estate next door.

Hedgerows reminiscent of the ones along Burroughs Lane flanked the drive leading up to the Montalone estate. If possible, the hedgerows here were even higher and denser, and the drive itself at least twice as long as Sheldrake's lane. Ariele felt relieved when she finally saw the manor ahead of her.

She brought her car to a stop where the driveway curved up to meet the yard. For a moment she just sat and looked at the manor. It was constructed of brick with narrow windows that were shuttered tight. The home reminded Ariele of a bleak fortress. It was a fitting comparison, considering the reclusive nature of the man who lived in it. Whatever hopes she had nurtured for meeting the man named Thomas Montalone died like embers in a cold rain.

Still, she hadn't come this far only to turn back without accomplishing at least part of her purpose. So she walked up to the front door and lifted the brass knocker. Ariele waited a couple of minutes. When no one answered, she knocked a second time.

At last the door swung open. On the other side stood a tiny woman in a black dress. She stared at Ariele through huge glasses that gave her a startled appearance, like that of an owl. "Yes? What can I do for you?"

Ariele said as calmly as she could, "My name is Ariele Harwood, and I'm the new owner of the Sheldrake estate. I need to speak with Mr. Montalone, please. It's about a very urgent matter."

"I'm sorry." The housekeeper made a quick, birdlike movement with her hand. "Mr. Montalone doesn't receive visitors." Her eyes darted to the book Ariele was holding. "If you would like to leave a message, I will relay it to Mr. Montalone for you."

"It's important that I speak with him myself," Ariele persisted.

"As I said, miss, that's impossible."

A sound came from somewhere within the manor. Was it a man's voice? The housekeeper turned abruptly, almost closing the door on Ariele. Then, after a moment, the woman returned. She stared at Ariele uncertainly. "Mr. Montalone will receive you in his study." She motioned for Ariele to follow her.

They entered a long, narrow corridor very similar to the downstairs hall at Sheldrake. The housekeeper led Ariele to a door at the end. "Here we are," she announced.

Ariele's first impression of the study was of a room where nothing had been disturbed in many years. A huge, ancient-looking desk commanded the center of the room. Bookcases lined one wall. On the far side of the room two easy chairs were placed close together. But Ariele's attention didn't linger long on the furnishings. Rather, it was drawn to the man who stood with his back to her at the room's impressive marble fireplace.

The man's hair was white now instead of blond, but Ariele saw that it was still thick and wavy. And though his broad shoulders were slightly stooped from age, the man was tall and well built, easily filling the tweed jacket and slacks that he wore. In one hand he held a poker with which he began to stir the ashes in the hearth.

Ariele cleared her throat. "Mr. Montalone?"

He didn't respond, only continued his task until he seemed satisfied that he was finished. Still, he didn't turn around. "So you are the new mistress of Sheldrake," he said in a voice that was deep and strong.

"Yes. I'm Ariele Harwood, Elizabeth Sheldrake's great-niece."

"I know. I watched you come across the yard." There was an audible sigh. "For a moment I thought that you *were* Elizabeth."

A lump rose in Ariele's throat; she swallowed it away. "I wasn't aware that we . . . resembled each other until I saw a photograph of her as a young woman."

"You are just as beautiful as she was."

Beautiful. Van had made a similar remark. Why didn't Thomas turn so that she could see his face? Was it because it would cause him too much pain to have to look at her? "I came today because I found some-thing at Sheldrake that belongs to you."

Thomas Montalone shook his head. "I can't imagine anything at Sheldrake that would belong to me now." The words sounded as if they had been wrenched from his heart. "You're aware that Eliza-beth and I were deeply in love."

"Yes. I discovered a locket that my aunt had worn. Your picture was inside the locket. I had no idea at first who you were, though I knew you must have been someone who was special to her. Then I found a book of sonnets. You had written an inscription in the front of it."

"*Sonnets from the Portuguese and Other Love Poems*," Thomas said softly. "I was planning to ask Elizabeth to marry me."

"But you never did."

"You know the reason, don't you?"

There was nothing but to be truthful with him. "My aunt's housekeeper, Emma, told me."

"Emma's a good woman. What did she say to you?"

"That there had been a tragedy, a fire. That a man was killed."

Thomas lowered his head. The silence in the room grew oppressive, the very air, it seemed, burdened with sadness. "Nearly fifty years," he said at last. "It has been nearly fifty years, and the nightmare is as terrifying as ever. In my sleep, every waking moment, what happened that night is with me. It will be with me until I take my last breath." The broad shoulders slumped visibly.

Ariele had an overwhelming urge to go to the older man, to tell him that he mustn't torture himself any longer. But what good would words of comfort do? Only Elizabeth's letter held any hope of offering him solace now. "That's why I'm here, Mr. Montalone. Because Elizabeth loved you."

Thomas gave a short, bitter laugh. "I've always wanted to believe it was so. That was another sort of dream."

"It wasn't just a dream. Elizabeth wrote you a letter before she died. I found it just today."

"A letter?" The older man stood erect again.

"Yes. It was in an envelope in Elizabeth's desk. I didn't know what was inside until I opened it." Ariele took a step forward. "The letter's rightfully yours. It and the book of sonnets."

Thomas picked up the poker and resumed stirring the ashes. "Would you . . .

be so kind as to lay them on my desk beside the morning paper."

Ariele didn't move at first, wishing again that he might turn and meet her eyes, let her know by his expression as well as his words that she had done the right thing in coming there. But he didn't move, and so she went to put the book on his desk. She left it open to the page where the letter and dried rose were placed. Then she prepared to leave. Pausing at the door, she glanced back at the older man. "Mr. Montalone, I want to thank you for granting me the privilege of meeting you." She turned away.

"Must you go already?"

The question riveted Ariele in place. "I thought that's what you wanted, Mr. Montalone."

"Please, just Thomas."

"And I'm Ariele."

"I owe you an explanation for my behavior, Ariele."

"You don't owe me anything, Thomas."

"I believe that I do. Come. We'll talk."

Ariele looked toward the fireplace. What she saw almost caused her to cry out in stunned surprise. Covering the right side of Thomas's face was a mask fashioned of black cloth. The mask concealed half of his forehead, his right cheek and most of his chin. There was just a small hole for his eye to see through.

The word *disfigured* came into Ariele's mind, and she surmised that Thomas had suffered burn injuries to his face in the fire that had killed Jess Walker. Yet she didn't find his appearance repulsive or frightening. Instead, the mask enhanced his features in some strange way and lent the older man a certain mysterious look.

Thomas brought a hand up to touch the mask. "I assume Emma didn't tell you about this."

"No."

He walked over to meet her. "Why don't we sit down, and I'll answer all your questions."

Ariele hesitated, uncertain, not wanting to put him through any more pain. Then her eyes met his. She saw the need in them. He had to tell her his story. So she accepted his invitation to take one of the chairs.

After he had seated himself in the other chair, Thomas began. The Walkers and the Montalones, he explained to her, owned the most prosperous estates in the Burroughs Valley, as the area was then called. Jeb Walker, Jess's father, was known for his cleverness and his ability to buy others' favor, which he used to gain political power. Jess, as the oldest son in the family, was being groomed to follow in his father's footsteps.

"Elizabeth and I knew each other nearly all of our lives," Thomas said. "We played together as children. By the time I was eighteen and Elizabeth sixteen, we'd fallen in love." He paused. "But Jess was used to getting his own way. Whatever he wanted, he took — by whatever means necessary. And what he wanted most was Elizabeth."

"She loved you."

"That gave Jess even more cause to pursue her. He hatched a scheme, threatened to stir up a scandal about Elizabeth and myself. And he had the cunning to carry it off." Thomas glanced away. "I couldn't bear for Elizabeth's reputation to be brought into question. I thought about the two of us running away together and getting married. But I had no money, no means of supporting a family at the time."

"Surely people wouldn't have believed his lies."

Thomas regarded her. "Jess had a certain charm. He also had the influence of the Walker name to back him up. I was sure I couldn't stop him, so when he asked me to meet him and talk things out man-to-man, I agreed, foolishly thinking I might be able to talk some sense into him."

Raising his hand to the mask, Thomas made some brief adjustment in it. Ariele averted her eyes, her heart filled with sympathy for the older man. "What happened?" she prompted gently.

"It was Jess who suggested that we meet at the barn on the old Litton estate. No one had lived there in years; there wasn't a house in miles of the place. It was the night of November 14th. The weather was blustery, the sky almost pitch-black with just a sliver of the moon showing."

Ariele easily saw it in her mind — the tops of the trees whipping in the wind, the ghostly outline of a ramshackle barn, the shadowy forms of the two men.

"Jess had a lantern," he continued. "Though the barn was little more than a shell of a building, he suggested we step inside, out of the wind. Ignoring common sense, I followed him in. I got a good look at him then. His eyes looked wild, and I realized he'd been drinking. I turned away from him, intent on getting out of there, but he grabbed my arm and swung me around. We exchanged words. Jess set the lantern down and challenged me to a fight.

He raised his fist at me; I put my arms up to defend myself. Then . . .” Thomas brought his hands to his face.

Ariele reached out to him, touching the rough tweed fabric of his coat. “This is too much for you, Thomas.”

Lowering his hands, he drew in a shuddering breath. “No. I must tell you the rest. Jess began to taunt me. Soon I was too angry myself to do any reasoning. So we fought. I landed a punch to his chin, and he staggered backward, just staring at me for a moment. Then he pulled a gun from his pocket and said he was going to kill me.”

“Jess had planned on *murdering* you?”

A hint of a smile crossed Thomas’s lips. “That seemed to be his intention. We were both young, inexperienced — and, I believe I can say now, scared. But Jess’s pride wouldn’t let him back down. I pleaded with him to be sensible. He answered by firing a shot over my head. Then somehow he bumped into the lantern. It toppled over and set a pile of old hay on fire.”

Thomas got up from his chair and began to pace. He walked the length of the room and back. At the desk he stopped and gazed down at the book of sonnets. He took the envelope and held it for a moment. Then he examined the rose. Finally, he returned to his chair.

"I shouted to Jess to get out of the barn," he went on in a subdued voice. "Instead, he aimed the gun at me and ordered me to turn around. I felt the heat of the fire on my face. I was certain I was about to be executed when all at once Jess lurched forward. He tripped, falling past me and into the flames. I grabbed for him, but . . ." Thomas bowed his head.

Ariele put her hand on top of his. "You did everything you could. Everything."

Thomas lifted his eyes; they stared hollowly into hers. "It was too late. Jess's clothes were on fire. He pleaded with me, begged me to save him. Perhaps . . . it would have been better if we both had perished."

"No! You mustn't say that." Ariele felt sick inside. It was as if, even in death, Jess Walker had the power to reach out from the grave and poison others' lives. "Thomas, I would call you a hero."

He gave a short, bitter laugh. "My dear child, a hero is one who saves another's life. And a hero doesn't run away like a coward."

"You left Burroughs Valley after that?"

"At the time it seemed I didn't have

much of a choice. Rumors were flying, folks saying I'd deliberately killed Jess. I was never brought to trial, but I'd already been tried and convicted in a lot of people's minds."

"Elizabeth couldn't have believed those rumors."

Thomas sighed. "I wasn't even sure of that at the time. Her father forbade her to ever see me again. Once she managed to send a note to me by way of the gardener. She asked me to meet her at the carousel on a certain night. I waited there for her until dawn, but she never came. I later learned that her father was sending her away, though I wasn't told where. Not long after, my own father suggested it might be in my best interests to go away for a while too. So I went to work on the railroad."

"Why did you come back?"

"I'd been gone for eight years when my father suddenly died. I was the only son in the family, and I felt a responsibility toward my mother and sisters. So I returned home — and I stayed."

"You and my aunt never saw each other again?"

"No."

The word hung heavily between them, and Ariele wondered if there was anything left for either of them to say. She made a move to get up from her chair. But Thomas's hand on her arm held her back.

"There is one other thing I have to tell you, Ariele."

"Yes?"

Thomas leaned forward, folding his hands together in front of him. "I'd been away only a short while when I received a piece of news. There was a young woman named Carrie who had grown up in the valley with Elizabeth, Jess, and myself. She and Jess saw each other for a time, but since he claimed to love Elizabeth, I never figured he had intentions toward Carrie. I was wrong. Jess had intentions, just not honorable ones."

"What do you mean?"

"Some months after Jess's death, Carrie had a child. Jess's son."

"He'd fathered a child by her?"

"Apparently so. Soon after the baby was born, she married another man. The two of them didn't have any children of their own, but the man gave the baby his name." Thomas paused. "Maybe you've heard of the name Winslow."

"Archer Winslow!" she exclaimed. "He's determined to buy Sheldrake."

Thomas's eyes narrowed. "You must be

careful, Ariele. He's Jess Walker's grandson."

A shiver passed through her. "Van told me to be careful," she said, more to herself than to Thomas.

"Van?"

"Van . . . that is, Mr. Caulfield. He was my aunt's attorney, the executor of her estate."

Thomas regarded her closely. "Do you trust Van Caulfield?"

"Yes." She said it without hesitation — and knew in her heart that it was the truth. "He told me something else, Thomas. I'd mentioned to him that I regretted never having the opportunity to know my aunt. He said it wasn't too late, that I could still get to know her if I gave myself the chance. He was right."

"Van sounds like a perceptive young man," Thomas said softly. "Am I right in believing that what you feel for him is more than mere trust?"

She looked away, unable to return his steady gaze. "Yes, you're right."

"And he's in love with you, as well, isn't he?"

The question triggered in her a storm of memories too fresh, too vivid, for her to examine rationally. Memories of Van, his hands framing her face, his fingers nestled intimately in her hair. *"I'm falling in love with you,"* he'd said.

"Your silence tells me a great deal, Ariele."

All at once Ariele felt unbearably warm. She rose swiftly from her chair and went over to where the bookcases stood. Her eyes scanned the titles without seeing them. Randomly she selected a volume from one of the shelves. Looking at it, she recognized the name. *"Destiny's Design* by Zachary McGuire," she said, turning to Thomas. "I've read this book. I loved the story."

Thomas came to stand beside her. "You did?"

"Yes. In fact, I've read all of his novels." She looked at Thomas. "I just wish this one had a happy ending."

"There are times when a sad ending is necessary." Thomas took the book from her and placed it back on the shelf. He was silent for a moment. "Would you accept advice from a foolish old man?"

"You are not foolish."

He met her eyes. "We won't argue the point, Ariele. But I sense that you are uncertain for some reason about the man you're in love with."

She shook her head. "It isn't Van. I mean . . . he's wonderful. It's just that I'd been comparing him to someone I'd dated before, someone who turned out not to be so wonderful. I realize now they aren't alike at all. Still, everything has been happening so fast between us. It's a little scary."

"Your past experience has made you cautious. That's not a bad thing, Ariele, to be cautious. But there are times when you must listen to your heart as well as your head." He squeezed her hand. "Don't allow uncertainty or fear to deprive you of the happiness you deserve, my child."

"Thank you," she whispered.

"Now," Thomas said with a smile, "I'll walk you out."

They slowly made their way down the hallway and through the foyer. At the front door, Ariele turned to Thomas.

"Will you come visit me again?" The question was asked with great dignity, but a certain sadness filled the older man's eyes.

Ariele smiled. "I plan to visit you again very soon."

His features relaxed. "I'm glad." He took her hand in his once more. "And now, Ariele, you'll take care, won't you?"

"I will."

Crossing the yard, Ariele stopped once to look back at Montalone Manor. She wasn't surprised to see that Thomas was gone and the front door closed tight. But she imagined that he was watching her from behind one of those shuttered windows, and she raised her hand in a wave to him before she went on to her car.

Chapter Thirteen

On arriving home, Ariele realized she was hungry. She hadn't taken time to fix herself something to eat before she'd hurried off to the Montalone estate. Now she decided that she'd make herself a sandwich from the sliced meat in the refrigerator.

Passing the parlor, she couldn't resist stopping at the doorway to look in. She took care not to touch so much as the door frame in case a fingerprint had been left on it. From what she could tell, nothing in the room had been tampered with except for the piano. The lid on the keyboard had been lifted, exposing the keys, and the little door where the music rolls were inserted was standing ajar.

It was easy for Ariele to picture Zelda there, her angular frame bent over the piano as she committed her mischief. The vivid image gave Ariele a chill, and she moved on down the hall to the kitchen.

As she prepared a roast beef sandwich, her mind became preoccupied with thoughts of Thomas Montalone. She was more than satisfied that she had done the right thing in taking the letter to him. Now she felt a kinship with her aunt that she would never have known if she hadn't taken the chance and gone to the Montalone estate. Thomas had done her a favor too. By his astute questions, he had forced her to come to terms with her feelings for Van. But was she ready to tell Van that she loved him? Yes, she was. And she was ready to send those old, destructive memories of Jerod packing for good.

Ariele wandered over to gaze out the window while she ate. Wide swatches of blue sky were visible where only clouds had been before. The sun would be shining soon.

The brightening weather gave Ariele an idea. It was early yet, just after three. Rather than sit around the house waiting for Van to come, she would go check on the merry-go-round, make sure it hadn't received any damage from the wind and rain. She ate the rest of her sandwich and finished the tidying-up of the kitchen that she'd begun the night before. Then she went out, testing the back door to make sure it was locked.

A short distance from the thicket Ariele spotted the tarp. It was just as she'd feared.

The canvas lay crumpled on the ground, completely removed from the merry-go-round. But as she drew closer, her sense of dismay changed to feelings of confusion. Something was terribly wrong about the scene.

Her nerves, more on edge than she'd realized, drew tighter. She told herself that she was overreacting, that the incident with the piano had sensitized her to anything that appeared even slightly amiss.

But no amount of reassurance could have prepared her for the horrifying sight that greeted her inside the thicket. Directly in front of her, propped against the carousel, was one of the wooden horses. It was *her* horse, Ariele saw as she moved closer — the one she had so meticulously painted. But it was barely identifiable as a horse at all. Its head had been ghoulishly lopped off and now lay at the animal's feet. And its body, a confection in pastels when she and Van had left it the day before, was hideously marred with red slashes and streaks.

For a dazed moment Ariele imagined that the red was blood. "Wooden horses don't bleed," she muttered to herself as she moved slowly around the animal. When she touched the animal's side, she recognized that the red substance was paint. It was dry, so the paint must have been applied some time ago.

She stared at the animal, disbelieving. Would she wake up and find she'd only dreamed it? Or was this real — like the piano playing in the night? After a moment she began to detect a pattern in the red streaks and slashes. Not just a pattern, but letters, writing of some sort. Her fingers traced the letters, spelling out the words: LEAVE SHELDRAKE OR DIE!

Ariele recoiled from the horse. Who would want to write something like that? Zelda Pilchard? It was possible that the woman knew about the carousel, since it had belonged to her half-sister. And the old crone was astute. Maybe she'd snooped around and found out the carousel was being renovated. But was she so desperate to get her hands on Sheldrake that she would stoop to decapitating wooden horses and scrawling death threats on them? Or was it another act of revenge?

Ariele's thoughts began to focus on someone else, someone who assuredly had the type of criminal mentality that would drive him to resort to any means necessary to snatch her estate away from her. Archer Winslow, she was certain, wouldn't blink

255

twice before setting out on a campaign of terror. Hadn't he already told her she'd be sorry if she held on to Sheldrake? Further, it was very possible that he had gotten away with murder once. What would prevent him from resorting to it again?

Other warnings came back to haunt her.

"You must be careful," Thomas Montalone had said.

"The owner of Winslow Farms is a dangerous man," Van had cautioned.

Despite her churning emotions, she told herself that she must stay calm and act rationally. Her first priority was to get back to the manor and phone the sheriff's office. She doubted it would be possible to reach Van. If she did by chance get through to him, what good would it do to tell him about the nightmarish events of the past twelve hours when he was too far away to come to her?

Before she left the thicket, Ariele made herself do a check of the rest of the merry-go-round. She found no other signs of damage — which somehow made the idea that her horse had been singled out for destruction even more disturbing.

As she passed through the crumbling remnants of the formal garden, the headless statue of Pan struck her as grotesque.

The rose arbor and bench held no romantic appeal now. Instead, the garden seemed almost menacing in its overgrown state, as if it harbored some sinister secret from the past.

At the point where the trails merged into one, Ariele slowed her steps without knowing why. Was it because she'd heard a sound in the brush? She listened intently. There was a noise, and she tensed in response. Was someone hiding in the bushes?

But the noise appeared to be coming from a spot very near her feet. Ariele looked down; at that instant a patch of brown raced past her toes. It took a minute for her to recognize the patch as a mouse. She caught sight of it just as it dived under a clump of ivy leaves.

She was about to start off again when the thought registered in her mind that something wasn't right about the little scene she'd just witnessed. Bending down, she soon honed in on what it was. Splatters of red spoiled the shiny green foliage of the ivy. *Paint,* she thought — the same type that had been applied to the horse. A brief inspection of the area revealed more splatters. They appeared to form a sort of path that paralleled the trail to the gardener's cottage.

Driven now by curiosity, Ariele started following the erratic path of paint drops. They took her straight to Denton's home and around the side of it to a door at the back.

Too stunned to do anything else, Ariele simply stood where she was. *Denton?* Was the gardener responsible for the death threat? That was impossible, wasn't it? Hadn't he gone to visit relatives? An image of him stealing across the dark lawn of the manor crept into her mind, and she shivered. Could he have come back, when she was asleep, to deface the horse?

Another possibility occurred to her. Might Denton have been set up? Archer Winslow had the motive, she knew, and the craftiness necessary to make it look like someone other than himself had committed the crime. Yet she couldn't shake the odd feeling that Denton might be as capable of penning a death threat as Archer.

Ariele tried the door to the cottage. It was unlocked, and she made a snap decision to go inside.

The room she stood in was dark and dingy. It was obviously a storage area. From the light coming in through the open doorway, she could make out various gardening implements hanging on hooks around the walls. Numerous smaller hand tools and assorted bottles with varied colored liquids in them occupied a table on one side of the room. Several bags of fertilizer were stacked on the opposite side, in a corner.

Ariele's attention soon became focused on the floor. Scattered across the worn, dirty boards was a small, but definite, trail of paint drops. They came to an end at the bags of fertilizer.

Feverishly Ariele began to drag the heavy sacks away from the wall. She pulled the last one free and looked into the corner, expecting to find a paint can. What she saw instead was a pair of black boots. She picked one of them up. It was scuffed and worn-looking, but otherwise unremarkable. Disappointed, she started to set the boot beside the other one when she noticed a tan-colored substance caked on its toe. Flecking off a bit of the substance, she deduced that it was mud.

The imprint left at the scene of the cut phone wires had been made by the toe of a shoe or boot. Ariele had more than a suspicion now that it had been made by the boot she held in her hand. There was only one way to know for sure. She would take the boot with her back to the manor and see if it matched the imprint.

Ariele set the boot aside and pushed the fertilizer bags into the corner. Her eyes scanned the room. What else might Denton have hidden there? The paint can, surely. If she could find it . . .

Her gaze came to rest on a small cabinet set in the wall across the room. Going over to it, she saw that it was padlocked. The lock was small. Could it be hammered open?

Ariele searched through the clutter of tools on the table and finally located a hammer. She struck the lock with it; on the third blow, the lock popped loose. Ariele threw the hammer back on the table and pulled open the cabinet door.

Should she have been shocked by what she saw inside? On the bottom shelf stood the alabaster bust of the young girl, her cupid's-bow mouth turned up in a frozen smile. On the middle shelf were the blue perfume vial and several inkwells. On the top shelf, assorted pieces of glassware were arranged in a crooked row.

Ariele slowly closed the cabinet door. So Denton, not the Pilchard sisters, had been responsible for the pilfering going on at the manor. What reason did he have for taking the items? Did he plan to sell them? That hardly mattered, she told herself as she picked up the boot. What she needed to do was get to a phone and call the proper authorities.

"Doing a little detective work, Miss Harwood?"

Ariele let out a startled cry at the sound of the low, gravelly voice. Her fingers let go of the boot; it fell with a thud to the floor. Turning around, she saw the figure of Denton in the doorway.

The gardener moved swiftly toward her. He reached out and grabbed her wrist. His fingers dug painfully into her flesh.

She had never gotten a good glimpse of Denton before. Now, in the stream of light from outside, she saw that his eyes looked pale and cold. They stared, unblinking, into hers. His skin was pale too, almost bloodless in appearance. *He's a brute,* she thought with rising fear, *the kind who thrives on hurting innocent people.*

Somehow she had to save herself. With a desperation born of instinct, she raised her foot and landed a kick to his shin. Denton only laughed and grasped her tighter. With a mighty effort she managed to wrestle her arm free. He caught it again, twisting it behind her back until she screamed in pain.

261

She tried to bite him. He hurled a curse at her and shoved her against the table.

Hovering over her, he taunted, "You think you're a match for me, Miss Harwood?" He pushed her down and brought out a length of cord from his pocket. He bound her wrists to the table leg with it. Then he took another piece of cord and lashed her ankles together.

Denton's face was even with hers. The sight of it sickened her. "You're not a gardener at all, are you?" she challenged in a voice that sounded braver than she felt. "Who are you? Why are you at Sheldrake?"

Denton gave a hoarse laugh. "I think I'm a fine gardener. But my real pleasure comes from scaring little ladies like you."

Trembling, she said, "You didn't answer my last question."

His impassive gaze held hers. "Save it for the boss."

The boss. With those two words, everything began to fall into place in Ariele's mind. The terrible truth of who had committed what crimes at Sheldrake — and why — became clear to her. "You mean Archer Winslow."

There was a flicker of life in the pale eyes. "The boss said you were smart, and here I'd only thought you were pretty." His lips curved in a colorless smile. "You'll be comfortable enough until he comes."

"Just what does Archer plan to do with me? He must be bright enough to know he can't get away with . . ."

"*Murder?*" Denton's voice wrapped seductively around the word.

Ariele turned away from him, but he seized her chin in his hand and made her face him again. "You got too curious for your own good, Miss Harwood." He shook his head. "It would have been fun taking care of you myself." He gave her head a jerk. Then he released her and stood up.

Covertly Ariele watched as Denton's lanky legs carried him to the door. He paused, and she feared that he might come back to her. But he went out instead, banging the door shut. She heard the sound of a key being turned in the latch.

Blackness closed in on Ariele. For a panicky moment she felt as if she couldn't breathe in the claustrophobic atmosphere of the lightless room. "Take a deep breath," she ordered herself. The effort made her chest hurt, but when she exhaled she could feel a slight easing of the tension that bunched her muscles in knots. One thing was imperative. She must keep her wits about her if she were to have any chance of surviving.

What were her chances? Realistically, they didn't look good. She was bound hand and foot and locked in a room where she could see nothing. Her captor had left, but it was an almost certain bet that he wouldn't be gone long. And when he returned, he would have Archer Winslow with him.

Ariele tested her bonds and found that she was able to wriggle her fingers a bit. It wasn't much, but she told herself to be encouraged by it. Picturing the table in her mind, she tried to visualize the various tools strewn about on it. Where had the hammer landed when she'd tossed it down? Was it beside the handsaw? Funny how something that seemed so inconsequential at the time now took on supreme importance. If only she could recall where she'd seen the saw, she might be able to use it to free herself.

Her immediate dilemma was how to reach the saw when it was on the tabletop and she was on the floor. She had an idea. Maybe she could jiggle the table and cause the saw to fall on the floor. Then she thought of the bottles. What if they toppled over too? Were there hazardous chemicals in them that might cause her harm?

Better to try to raise herself up so that her face was at table level, she decided. Even though she couldn't see in the dark, she might be able to literally nose around and locate the saw that way. She wriggled her fingers again in an effort to further loosen the cord. It wouldn't budge. Still, she discovered she had enough slack to allow her to grasp hold of the table leg and begin to inch her hands upward along its rough surface.

Working at a snail's pace, Ariele had to remind herself to be patient, that to act hastily could result in disaster. Her breath came in short gasps from the intensity of her efforts. Beads of perspiration broke out on her forehead and ran down her cheeks like tears. Finally, she was able to attain a squatting position. Just a little farther and she would be face-level with the tabletop.

Her legs shook from the weight she was putting on them. She shifted slightly, seeking a more stable stance. Then disaster struck. It started with a small vibration in the table that set her off balance. As she frantically sought to regain her leverage against the table leg, she heard a fatal splintering sound, and the leg gave way, snapping in two.

Ariele went tumbling backward. At the same instant havoc reigned as the table tipped over, and the tools and bottles went crashing to the floor. For what seemed hours she heard the sound of glass smashing and shattering around her. Miraculously, none of the flying shards hit her face.

At last, silence fell over the room again. Shaking and near tears, Ariele assessed her situation. She discovered that, though they were still tied, her hands were attached to the piece of table leg that had broken free. Little good that would do her, she knew, since she was no doubt sitting in a sea of razor-sharp glass. How could she hope to move even an inch without risking cutting herself badly?

Ariele discovered that there was another problem. A strange smell filled the air, which she identified as ammonia. It choked her and made breathing next to impossible. Her eyes began to water.

The utter darkness of the room, the broken glass, the suffocating odor was too much for her. Despair settled over her like a shroud. Then all at once she began to laugh. *Now I'm getting hysterical,* she thought. Would Archer and Denton laugh too when they found her already dead? Or would Archer feel cheated out of the pleasure of killing her?

She laughed all the harder. Her body shook; she drew in great gulps of air, but that only made her cough more. Then she stopped — stopped the laughing, the coughing, the crying. For an instant she imagined that she'd heard someone calling her name. *This is worse. Now I'm hallucinating.* But she heard the sound again, and she was certain. Someone *was* calling to her. Impossibly, it was Van!

Drawing in the biggest breath she could, she screamed, "I'm here, Van! I'm here."

"Ariele!" His voice, urgent, desperate, came to her from the other side of the door.

"The door's . . . locked," she rasped.

"Stand away from it, Ariele. I'm breaking in."

She had only enough breath left to warn, "Be careful. There's . . . broken glass."

There were a couple of hard thuds. Then it was as if the room was caving in on her as the door exploded open. The next thing Ariele knew she could see light, then Van standing over her. He threw something aside that he held in his hand. Bending down, he whispered her name. Then he lifted her in his arms and carried her outside, where he made short work of untying the lengths of cord binding her wrists and ankles.

For some minutes she could only lie in Van's arms, coughing. "Breathe slowly, deeply," he ordered, and she did. After a little she found that the burning in her throat and lungs had begun to ease. Her eyes were clearing too.

She looked up at him. He was dressed in his black leather jacket and a white dress shirt — ready to take her to dinner, she thought. But now his face was creased with worry lines. Touching his cheek, she said, "How did you know I was here?"

The anxious expression gave way to a slight smile. "I didn't . . . exactly." He grew serious again. "All day I couldn't get you out of my mind, couldn't shake the uneasy feeling I had that you were in danger." He paused to brush a kiss across her forehead. "I was on my way to Sheldrake when I thought I spotted Denton's car on the road. That puzzled me since he was supposed to be away. After you didn't answer my knock at the manor, I figured you were at the carousel."

"Then you've . . . seen the horse?"

"Yes." Van cradled her closer. "As soon as I saw the death threat, I had a gut feeling that Denton had something to do with it."

"Denton's not alone in this, Van. He's working for Archer Winslow."

Van looked grim. "I should have guessed that."

"Wait until you see what I found in the storage room."

"Incriminating evidence?"

Ariele managed a smile. "Only a boot with mud caked on its toe. Not to mention the alabaster bust, a perfume vial, and several inkwells." Her lips trembled. "I have so much to tell you, Van."

"And I want to hear all of it. But right now we've got to get back to the manor and phone the sheriff's office." He regarded her. "Do you think you can walk?"

"Yes," she said with more confidence than she felt. "But couldn't you make the call on your cellular phone?"

Van looked rueful. "I don't have it — or my pager — with me. I didn't want our dinner to be interrupted."

"How about using Denton's phone?"

"The cottage doesn't have one."

"Oh." It seemed they were out of options. "Well, let's go then." She started to get up, but her knees buckled, threatening to throw her down again.

Van's arm came around her waist to support her. "I'll help you." He raised her to her feet. Together, they took a few slow steps forward. "This isn't working," he said against her hair. "I'll carry you."

"I'll be fine," she insisted. But despite her protest, Van lifted her in his arms. They stared into each other's eyes. "I love you," she said, pressing a kiss into the hollow at the base of his neck.

"I love you," he whispered.

"What a touching sight."

Van froze in place. Ariele let out a cry at the sound of Archer Winslow's voice. She turned her head to find him approaching. Denton was with him.

As Archer advanced on them, Ariele saw that his mouth was twisted in a cruel smile. In his hand he held a revolver. "This is not quite how I anticipated things would turn out." He pointed the gun at Van.

Van's hold on Ariele tightened protectively. "You've hanged yourself this time, Winslow," he warned.

"I wouldn't be too sure of that, my friend." His words sounded confident, but Ariele saw that his hand shook a little where he held the revolver. He came a menacing step closer. "Don't forget. I always come up a winner."

"Not this time," Van responded tersely.

Archer's gaze moved from Van to Ariele. "Oh, yes, this time too."

Ariele sensed that, for all his bravado, Archer was uncertain. No doubt, he had counted on simply frightening her into fleeing her estate. Now he had two captives on his hands.

"I'll simply have to make a change in my plans, that's all." His eyes were glued on Ariele. "I'm certain Miss Harwood is just *dying* to take a ride on that motorcycle of yours, Van." He gave a short laugh; his eyes glowed with dark excitement. "Yes . . . the two of you are about to go for a jaunt in the country. And I know the perfect spot. Sherwood Bluff." His gaze suddenly shifted to Van. "What a shame you'll miss that wicked curve. Such a nasty fall to take." He shook his head. "It'll be the talk of the town. That is, how you and Miss Harwood died in an accident due to your negligence. Too bad . . ."

Ariele heard no more. The words *"motorcycle . . . curve . . . accident"* spun wildly through her mind, and something in her snapped. She no longer felt weak, but strong. Screaming until it seemed her lungs would burst, she gave Archer a mighty push. Her elbow hit his ribs, and

271

he staggered, momentarily stunned.

"What the . . . ," he stammered.

Van was on him in an instant. What he did to Archer next, Ariele was helpless to say. Whatever it was, the gun went sailing out of Archer's hand, and Archer crumpled to the ground. He lay there, eyes closed and mouth open.

From behind her, Denton cursed. He jumped on Van's back. Ariele clawed at the gardener's shirt, pounded on his arms, his head. Denton easily threw her off.

Struggling to her feet, she watched as Van and Denton scuffled. Denton pummeled Van's chest and arms. Ariele screamed again. Denton turned his head toward her. At that instant Van's fist made contact with the gardener's jaw. Ariele heard the decisive crack of knuckle meeting jawbone, saw Denton go sprawling backward on the ground.

"Quick," Van commanded her. "Get me the cord."

She snatched up both pieces of it. Van rolled Denton over so that the gardener was facedown. Then he bound Denton's hands together. "We need more rope," Van called over his shoulder.

Sidestepping the broken glass, Ariele spied a coil of rope hanging on one of the wall hooks. She took it down and triumphantly started outside with it.

Her feeling of elation soon fled. To her horror, she saw that Archer had gotten to his feet. He was lurching toward Van, who still knelt over Denton. She yelled a warning to Van, but Archer clearly had the advantage.

Ariele went on a frenzied search for something to use as a weapon. She found what she needed in a piece of metal pipe that lay inside the storage room door. It must have been what Van had cast aside when he'd broken in.

Gripping the pipe in her hands, she went after Archer. She heard him mumbling and cursing. His fists were raised, ready to launch an assault on Van. Ariele took aim and swung the pipe full force against the backs of his legs.

Archer reeled forward; he grabbed at his knees, moaning in pain. Van jumped on him and delivered a blow to his face that sent him tumbling in a heap beside Denton.

Ariele fetched the coil of rope. Van used part of it to secure Archer's hands and feet. The rest he used to bind the two men together. "There," he said, smiling. "That ought to hold our criminals for a while."

Ariele smiled too, but it was a watery smile. She reached for Van just as he stretched out his arms to her. She collapsed into his embrace. He murmured words of love and comfort to her. She kissed his forehead and nose, and soothed a small bruise on his right cheek. His shirt was soiled with grass and dirt stains; a healthy growth of chest hair peeked out where the top two buttons of his shirt had come open. Ariele laid her hand there; his heart beat strong and steady beneath her fingertips. "Where did you learn to fight like that?" she asked.

Van gave a small laugh. "Amateur boxing used to be another one of my hobbies." When Ariele started to withdraw her hand from him, he caught it and held it against his chest a moment longer. Then he buttoned his shirt and located Archer's gun. "I'll guard the prisoners," he told her, "while you phone the authorities."

Ariele started off, then stopped. She looked back at Van. "Archer won't get off so easily this time, will he?"

Van grinned at her. "No, I don't think that he will."

Chapter Fourteen

It seemed to Ariele that the whole Burroughs County sheriff's office had descended on her estate. There was the sheriff himself, a tall, rugged-looking man named John Monroe. Then there were the sheriff's detective and at least a half dozen deputies.

After Archer and Denton were hauled off in the back of one of the deputies' cruisers, the sheriff and his detective took statements from Ariele and Van. The detective dusted for fingerprints in the parlor and hallway and around the outside of the window by the staircase. When a partial print was found on the piano, Ariele was glad that she'd had enough presence of mind to steer clear of the parlor until the authorities had arrived.

An investigation was also made by the officers of the gardener's cottage and the carousel. Anything that might be considered pertinent evidence was gathered. The investigation was finally brought to a conclusion around ten o'clock. Before he left, Sheriff Monroe informed Ariele and Van that he and the detective would be back the next afternoon.

Ariele closed the front door on the officers and turned to Van. "I'm impressed with the sheriff. He appears to run a very efficient department."

"He does," Van confirmed.

They stood together quietly for a moment. The manor seemed to enfold them in its silence, and Ariele felt comforted by it. She was also comforted by Van's presence beside her. "Would you like something to eat?" she asked him.

He smiled. "Now that you mention it, yes, I would."

Before they were out of the foyer, a rap sounded at the door.

"Now what?" They said it in unison, then laughed.

Ariele opened the door. One of the deputies was on the porch. He tipped his hat to her. "Sorry to bother you, Miss Harwood, but I found this by the door." He trained a flashlight on a parcel that he held in his hand. "It has your name on it." He gave the package to her.

"Thank you," she said absently, her eyes on the paper-wrapped parcel as she closed the door.

"What's that?"

Ariele looked at Van. "I have no idea." She tore off the wrapping. Inside was a book. She held it to the light. "*Destiny's Design*," she said with wonder.

Van stood very near. "What is *Destiny's Design*?"

"A novel." She ran her hand over the book's smooth brown cover. "It belonged to Thomas Montalone."

"The man Elizabeth was in love with."

Ariele nodded slowly. "I was at his home today, and I saw this on a shelf."

Van took hold of her chin, forcing her to look at him. "You visited Thomas Montalone?"

She smiled. "That was one of the things I was so eager to tell you." Opening the book to the first page, she let out a loud gasp of surprise. The novel had been autographed. "Zachary McGuire," she read aloud. "A.k.a. Thomas Montalone." She clasped hold of Van's arm. "Do you know what this means? Thomas Montalone is a novelist! Zachary McGuire is just a pseudonym."

Van traced Thomas's bold signature. "It looks like you've got a very special book to add to your library."

"Yes, I do," she said, her eyes misting over with tears.

"Why don't we see what we can find in

the kitchen to eat?" Van suggested softly. "Then we'll sit in the parlor and you can fill me in on the details of your day."

They put the book on a table in the parlor and went on to the kitchen. Ariele fixed a roast beef sandwich for Van and a turkey sandwich for herself. She put the sandwiches on a tray with bowls of Emma's fruit salad and mugs of hot tea that Van prepared from some tea bags he'd found on a shelf.

Van carried the tray into the parlor. As they ate in a leisurely fashion, Ariele asked him how his interview had gone.

"Good," he replied. "Now I want to hear about your visit with Thomas Montalone, though I would like to know first why you didn't call me as soon as you heard the piano playing in the night."

"I didn't want to wake you," she said simply.

Van's eyes narrowed, as if he might be angry. But when he spoke, his voice was tenderly protective. "You know that's exactly what I would have wanted you to do."

"Yes," she acknowledged. Then she smiled. "Actually, I thought I handled myself quite well under the circumstances. I was even brave enough to initiate a fight with Zelda Pilchard. Or so it seemed at the time."

Van held up his hand. "Wait a minute! Fight?" He looked bewildered. "You never said anything about a fight with Zelda when you gave John your statement."

Ariele couldn't keep from laughing. "No, because I would have died from embarrassment if I'd told him." She then related her tale of the wrestling match she'd had with the curtain.

Van chuckled. But he grew serious again as she went on to tell him about her discovery of the letter that prompted her visit to the Montalone estate. She described the older man to Van, sharing with him the details of the love affair that ended in tragedy for Thomas and her aunt.

"So Archer's grandfather tried to kill Thomas," Van said thoughtfully. "You know, you've got quite a story yourself now to tell Thomas."

"Yes, and I can't wait, though since he gets the newspaper, he'll probably read about it there first." She turned introspective. "I hope you can meet him someday, Van."

"I hope so too."

"Thomas is very intuitive." Ariele's eyes went to the book. "When I happened to mention your name in conversation, he discerned right away how I felt about you."

She turned back to Van. "He could see that I was in love with you, and he helped me to come to terms with my feelings."

Van took her empty dishes and stacked them together with his. He reached for her hand and kissed it. "Then Thomas Montalone has my deepest gratitude." He gazed at her, smiling, for a moment. "This wasn't quite what I had in mind for us tonight, Ariele. Imagine a cozy French restaurant that used to be a farmhouse. It's tucked up in the hills and has a terrific view. There are linen cloths and fresh flowers and candles on the tables. It's a romantic place, a place with ambiance. And the food's not shabby, either."

"Sounds enchanting," Ariele agreed. "But right now I'm finding the parlor to be an extremely romantic place, a place with ambiance."

Van cupped her shoulders in his hands. He touched his forehead to hers. "I'm glad you think so," he whispered, "because I have something extremely romantic to say to you."

A quiver went through Ariele, a response both to his nearness and his words. "What is that?"

"Just that I'm deeply in love with you and I can't imagine living my life without you." He pulled away from her briefly to reach into his pants pocket. "I'd planned on giving this to you over dessert." He pressed a small white box into her palm.

With trembling fingers, Ariele opened the box. Inside was one of the most gorgeous engagement rings she had ever seen. It was set with a large, heart-shaped diamond solitaire. "Van . . ." She couldn't get past his name.

"I took a risk, Ariele — a risk that you would say you'll marry me." His smile was tentative. "Will you?"

She realized those were the words she'd been longing to hear. And her answer was to throw her arms around his neck and bring her mouth to his in an ardent kiss.

"I'll take that as a yes," he said with a grin when the kiss ended. He took the ring and put it on the appropriate finger. By chance it fit perfectly. "I love you, Ariele."

"I love you, Van."

His arms went around her and she cuddled against him. She stared at the ring for a moment, thinking how right it looked nestled on her finger.

Van spoke first. "There's one thing I want to make clear to you. Whatever you decide to do with Sheldrake is fine with me. If you want to keep the estate, that's fine. If you'd rather sell it, that's okay too. I won't even protest if you choose to give the place away for a song."

Ariele regarded him. "I thought you were so eager for me to keep Sheldrake."

"I was. I *am*," he admitted. "But I have to confess that I had an ulterior motive." His gaze focused on her lips. "I wanted you from the moment I saw you, Ariele. I hoped that if you hung around, you might fall for me too."

"Well, your plan worked, Mr. Caulfield." She playfully traced the outline of his lips with her finger. "But if you wouldn't mind, I'd like to try my hand — our hand, that is — at transforming the manor into a bed-and-breakfast inn. How does The Carousel Inn sound to you?"

"The Carousel Inn," he repeated. "That sounds just about perfect." His mouth skimmed her brow; his hands slid over her back. "We'll make a great team, don't you think?"

"Mmm, a great team," she murmured.

"I would say all of this calls for a celebration."

"We could go to dinner tomorrow night."

"We will," he promised.

What were his lips doing to her neck, her

ear? Before she lost herself completely in the pleasurable sensations he was creating, Ariele pulled away from him a little. "Promise me something, Van."

His eyes were half closed. "Anything."

"Promise you'll take me for a ride soon on The Litigator."

Van's eyes opened. "You're serious, aren't you?"

"Completely."

"No fears?"

She hesitated for the barest fraction of a second. Then she said, "No fears." And she meant it.

"Then I'll take you, Ariele."

"How about first thing tomorrow?"

"Yes," he whispered against her cheek. "First thing tomorrow."

About the Author

Marilyn Prather graduated from New Mexico University with a B.S. degree in elementary education. She enjoys writing poetry as well as stories. She lives in Fort Myers, Florida, with her husband, David, and three cats.

The employees of Thorndike Press hope you have enjoyed this Large Print book. All our Thorndike and Wheeler Large Print titles are designed for easy reading, and all our books are made to last. Other Thorndike Press Large Print books are available at your library, through selected bookstores, or directly from us.

For information about titles, please call:

(800) 223-1244

or visit our Web site at:

www.gale.com/thorndike
www.gale.com/wheeler

To share your comments, please write:

Publisher
Thorndike Press
295 Kennedy Memorial Drive
Waterville, ME   04901